What's Sp
For Murder?

D. A. Blake

Another book by
D. A. Blake
is "What's Italian
for
murder"
It is equally as good
as this one.

www.publishnation.co.uk

Chapter One

February 14

Sarah Johnson swore loudly as she saw the blood running down her finger towards the palm of her hand, a rich, deep crimson, unexpectedly copious. As a child, she had often gazed at the veins under the surface of her skin, and for years had believed that she might one day catch a glimpse of the dark blue blood she was convinced was flowing around her body; perhaps in that nanosecond after the gash, before the oxygen in the air turned it red. Aristocratic aspirations had played no part whatsoever in this fruitless quest of Sarah's; just a misplaced scientific fascination. As she grew older, and science lessons had categorically dashed all her futile hopes, Sarah was glad that she had never confided in her peers. She didn't like to look foolish. The notion that she should be belittled had always been abhorrent to her. She liked to have the upper hand, to be in the know. In order to achieve this, she had learnt to play her cards close to her chest; her intentions invariably remained undisclosed. She knew how to hide her weaknesses and present a perfect front. A front that was intentionally daunting, designed to intimidate any prospective opponent.

Sarah winced and reached for some kitchen roll, a pained expression on her face. Dabbing hurriedly at the cut, then holding her hand in the air, she did her best to carry on with what she was doing. Chopping cucumber was just not her forte. Or tomatoes. Or anything else for that matter. She was never going to be a domestic goddess, or an earth mother for that matter. The thought of fun-filled, flour-covered baking sessions with her young son, Oliver, filled her with dread. Even warming up fish fingers and chips in the oven was getting her hot and bothered. What had been the point of that yoga session earlier, she wondered? Placing the chopped food onto a brightly coloured plastic plate with one hand, or at least the bits of food that weren't splashed red, she could almost feel the cortisol flooding her bloodstream. Some of that stress hormone was probably trickling down her finger right now, she thought.

Sarah should really have been on a call with the New York office. She was used to working late into the evening. She didn't mind. She loved her job. She loved the travelling that came with it. And she loved the power too. She'd had to fight to get to where she was today. Being Chief Financial Officer for a large American company meant long hours and a lot of hard work. But it certainly paid the bills. She'd already bought this house, as an investment more than anything, long before she'd met Anthony. She hadn't lived in it initially. So the rental income, as well as her burgeoning career, had meant that she was pretty comfortably off, even before they'd decided to set up home here together, restoring the house to its former glory. They'd managed to do plenty of renovation work already. The proceeds from her flat had certainly helped there. She'd had a gorgeous little pad right at the top of Richmond Hill, moments away from the park gates. It had been ridiculously expensive, considering you couldn't really swing a cat in there. But that view from her tiny balcony down towards the river had been worth every penny.

Her money had also given them the dream wedding they'd both always wanted. No expense had been spared to create that once-in-a-lifetime moment, a magical exchange of vows, just the two of them, barefoot on white sand, the Caribbean Sea lapping at the shore nearby. The absence of guests, all those seldom-seen aunties and envious friends, would make it all the more special, Anthony had insisted. They could have a wonderfully romantic, and utterly lavish, time instead. Which they did. And he'd been right. It had been glorious.

As was often the case recently, Luciana had popped out for five minutes. Nearly two hours ago. What was the point of having an au pair if she wasn't around at tea-time?

'Mummy, you said a naughty word,' came Olly's voice from the other end of the spacious open-plan room. He lay sprawled on a wide corner sofa, his eyes fixed on the large television attached to a wall. The vivid animated characters on the screen provided the only hint of colour in this minimalist, not

2

particularly child-friendly, setting; the vast white walls were just crying out for sticky fingerprints really. Sarah glanced across from where she stood reluctantly clearing up and laughed. 'I was talking about sheets. I need Luciana to put some clean sheets on your bed.'

The bi-fold doors that ran across the back of the entire room reflected the environment somewhat unfamiliar to Sarah. Bespoke pale grey kitchen cupboards lined one wall. An American fridge-freezer stood tucked in beside them, an ice-dispenser breaking up the floor-to-ceiling steel glinting under the spotlights in the ceiling; a gleaming aga sat within a large inglenook fireplace, a constant source of heat in addition to the underfloor heating that kept the white, glossy tiles so warm underfoot.

'Mummy, when's Daddy going to be back? He's always going away.'

'I know, sweetie. It's his job. It won't be for long. He only left this morning, didn't he?' She glanced at the huge vase of red roses and the two Valentine's cards on her kitchen island. There were a dozen roses, she knew that. She'd counted them playfully with Olly when she'd put them into water at breakfast time. Anthony and Olly had been sitting on bar stools eating their toast, still in pyjamas, their two identical mops of curly black hair as yet untamed. Sarah had pretended not to notice when Anthony had slathered an extra-thick layer of chocolate spread on the small pieces of toast that he'd carefully cut up for his little boy. Her husband always liked to make sure he spent a little quality time with their son before he headed off on yet another stint away from home.

In theory, their au pair oversaw Olly's breakfast; in practice, that didn't always happen. Luciana had been yet to make an appearance, though there'd been a lot of showering and hair-drying going on. Rather excessive for the school-run maybe, but then she imagined that twenty-two-year-old Colombian girls had standards to maintain. Anyway, that morning it had given Olly some precious one-to-one time with his often elusive father.

The television programme ended and, still on the sofa, Olly bounced up onto his knees, waving some cardboard around. 'I can't wait to show Daddy the sword I made today. I think I'm

3

going to make one for him too. Then we can play soldiers and see who gets killed first.' He began to thrust his makeshift sword in different directions. 'Mummy, in real fighting, does a proper knife go in easily, or do you have to really push it in?'

Sarah frowned and leant down to remove the fishfingers from the oven. They were burnt of course. She really didn't have a clue how to use the aga. She hated it if the truth be told, but it had come with the house and it seemed a shame to get rid of it.

The sound of a key in the lock had Sarah removing her apron and grabbing her coat.

'Luciana?' she called.

'Hi, sorry I was so long. I didn't look at the time.'

Sarah took in the short skirt and the unsubtle shade of lipstick. At least the girl had been sensible enough to wear some sort of jacket, she supposed.

'Well, you're back now. I've started Olly's tea. Can you take over? I'm sure you'll do a far better job than me. Sleep tight, Olly. Love you.'

And with that, she was out of the front door.

Luciana had been out and had her fun. It was her turn now.

Chapter Two

February 15

Michael Winterbottom stood patiently near the lifts of the large three-star hotel that he had worked at for the last two years. The third floor, like the other three floors, was quiet at this time of the morning. Most guests were already out and about. The grey men in their grey suits had scuttled off to their meetings, their hastily-eaten breakfasts half finished. The expensively groomed corporate women had all strutted off too, a mobile phone clamped to their ear, their overly loud voices announcing their imminent arrival, barking instructions in the meantime.

They didn't get many tourists at Lottan Lodge in Lower Haddelton. Parts of the town itself were pretty enough, with some lovely restaurants and cafés, and a number of quaint antique shops. The shopping centre was a little bland maybe, no different from a thousand other shopping centres, but there were plenty of decent shops. You could normally find what you were looking for. Unfortunately, the office blocks, while not exactly dominating the skyline, did nothing to add to the character of the place.

Lottan Lodge sat slightly away from the town centre, along the edge of the river Thames. It was actually a rather pleasant location. Some of the rooms had lovely views out over the water, and there was a simply-furnished terrace where guests could sit outside if they had the time or the inclination. Very few did. There were a few pretty pubs nearby, and great walks along the towpaths, not to mention easy access to the sprawling parks in the area. Hampton Court Palace lay further along the river in one direction, and Richmond could be visited if you went the other way. But, with a thirty-minute train ride needed to reach central London, the hotel was just a little too far away from the bright lights of the capital to warrant any length of stay unless you had some other business here.

Michael had originally raised his eyebrows at the couples turning up with desk lamps, duvet covers and tins of baked beans. Not, as it turned out, guests concerned about potential failings in the hotel's facilities. Rather, parents replenishing the supplies of their offspring occupying the town's university accommodation. Judging by the new blocks going up, he suspected that these students' rooms were probably somewhat superior to the rooms in the hotel.

They all knew that Lottan Lodge was looking a little tired these days, although Michael suspected that he'd be long gone by the time anything was done about it. He couldn't care less, if he was honest. He didn't take any pride whatsoever in working for this particular hotel. It was merely a stepping stone, a means to an end. He knew that, even if they spruced the place up to the nines, it would still pale in comparison with where he was heading.

Michael looked at his watch. Where on earth was George? He had better things to do than hang around third-floor corridors at half past ten in the morning. The receptionist they'd recently employed was proving to be pretty awful and he really wanted to be down there keeping an eye on her. She just seemed so unsuited to the job. He couldn't make her out really. It was so strange. She'd been such an unlikely candidate for the role. She'd had very little experience in the hotel industry for a start. Sophie was clearly a very bright girl with a good degree from a decent university under her belt. She'd travelled the world, spending time in various countries, teaching English or working in bars. Which is where her experience in hospitality came in. She could obviously take an order for a cocktail in at least four different languages, but he just wasn't sure how motivated she was about checking businessmen and women into their rooms in a bland hotel in Lower Haddelton. She really wasn't going to have the opportunity to use her languages here. And she really didn't seem to have much in common with any of the other staff.

Michael had tried to be polite, but in all honesty, he had very little interest in her epic backpacking trips around South America or Vietnam. In fact, he seemed to have to spend much of his time with her explaining, yet again, how the booking system or the telephone connections worked. It astonished him how someone so academic could have such little common sense. Something didn't seem to quite add up, actually. He couldn't quite put his finger on it. Michael had had significant reservations when they'd interviewed her, and so far, he was being proved right. But they'd been a bit desperate, caught out like that when Fabian had left.

God, he missed Fabian. He'd been so professional, so charming; he always went the extra mile. Michael had loved it when their shifts had coincided. In fact, he'd often made it his business that they did. He'd so enjoyed their little chats on quiet evenings, giggling about guests' demands, gossiping about the other hotel staff, bemoaning the lack of nightlife in Lower Haddelton. They'd often talked about the idea of going into London together for a night out. Michael had come up with lots of great suggestions. But it had never seemed to happen. He'd tentatively tried to delve into Fabian's personal life, tried to discover more about this handsome young French man. But he was clearly a private chap by nature. He'd always been a little reticent. He was never particularly forthcoming about his life outside the hotel. Michael imagined that he probably didn't have much of a life when he wasn't at work. He couldn't have known many people over here after such a short amount of time in the country; he'd been here in England for less than a year. He knew that he'd been going to English lessons at a local college once a week. Perhaps he'd made some friends there. Maybe they'd been quite a lively bunch, an international crowd, all Austrian au pairs and Spanish waiters. He used to get quite jealous thinking about it. Though he had to say, Fabian's English had come on leaps and bounds. Michael liked to think that he'd had something to do with that.

It was such a shame that he'd gone back to Paris at such short notice like that. They hadn't even had the chance to say goodbye properly, swap addresses, make tentative plans to meet up at some point. Michael had always wanted to visit Paris. He'd been picturing them strolling along the banks of the Seine in the sunshine, exploring the cobbled streets of Montmartre, relaxing in the Tuileries Garden after a lengthy stint at the Louvre. Fabian would know all the authentic, out of the way bistros and cafés where the locals ate. He'd laugh fondly at Michael's schoolboy French and at his reaction when trying *escargots* for the first time. They'd agree to make it a regular thing. After all, Paris and London were so close.

When Hattie from Accounts had mentioned Fabian's unexpected departure in passing, before George had found him to let him know, he had to admit he'd been dumbfounded. Flabbergasted. He'd had to pop into the toilets to compose himself. Even now, he still hadn't quite got to the bottom of it. He didn't think George was any more in the picture than he was.

George was the General Manager of Lottan Lodge, and seemed to be running late that morning. He and Michael were due to be carrying out some routine room inspections. Just to make sure that the Housekeeping team were not letting the side down.

George Henderson was a nice enough boss, Michael would concede, but, my goodness, he wasn't particularly on the ball these days. He was getting too old for all of this. All the running around. All the troubleshooting. Not that Michael was after his job. No, he was merely biding his time, getting experience, working his way up. And he was doing well. Becoming Front of House Manager a couple of years ago at the age of thirty had been quite an achievement.

Of course, he certainly wanted to be a General Manager. But not here. Not out in the sticks in some three-star chain hotel. Nothing exciting ever happened here. Nobody of interest ever set foot in this boring, non-descript establishment. They never even had the local press on their doorstep, never mind paparazzi from all over the world.

No, Michael had his eye on Mayfair. Somewhere discreet but sumptuous. Private but grand. Preferably favoured by Hollywood A-listers and minor Royalty. He'd picture himself offering quiet, knowing congratulations on that recent Oscar nod, utterly at ease with the glamour and stardom he dealt with on a daily basis; diplomatically greeting the young woman, or man, on someone's arm, having chatted politely to that person's perfectly pleasant wife just a month or two previously. He'd know which flowers to have in the room, which type of water was a must, and what sort of pillows were preferred. He would understand that nothing else would do. He would know, from experience, that there would be hell to pay if things weren't just so. The grateful hotel would rely upon his effortless professionalism to save the day time after time.

And, of course, he would always make sure that it was he who would be waiting to greet all these distinguished guests under the smart canopy covering the polished steps at the front of the hotel, composed and dignified in his beautifully tailored suit. He'd place a practised guiding arm behind them as they headed up towards the gleaming glass doors bearing the hotel's initials, as though to protect them from the glare of all those flashing lights, all those loud, prying questions. He'd be there to look after them for the duration of their stay, to ensure that their every need was met. He'd become a trusted acquaintance. They'd remember his name, of course. In fact, he'd probably be on first name terms with many of them.

When it came to Royalty, he'd done his research, of course. He knew exactly how to make the correct bow to a member of the Royal family. He'd practised the slight nod of the head many a time in front of his mirror, taking care to keep the rest of his body upright. Bending from the waist would look so foolish. He'd read that it was a massive faux pas to say 'Pleased to meet you' to the Royals. Because of course you were pleased to meet them. Yet 'How do you do?' just sounded ridiculous coming from him. 'Hello' was meant to be okay, though it did seem a little over-familiar. He'd soon learn, he imagined.

Michael glanced up the long, wide corridor that led away from the lifts, lined all the way with closed doorways at regular intervals. A dark green patterned carpet stretched out in front of him, clashing somewhat with the garish framed prints on the walls. The signs to the fire escape complemented the carpet better than the pictures did, he noted. Still, he wasn't responsible for the aesthetics of the place.

The corridor was silent apart from the rattle of an approaching trolley, recently emerged from one of the doorways, piled high with cleaning products and fresh towels. He nodded to the maid. Though not in a Royal way, of course. 'Hello, Dolores,' he called to her, raising his voice just a little, suspecting a touch of deafness, apart from everything else. His tone was detached, perfunctory.

'Good morning, Mr Winterbottom,' the maid replied warmly with a smile, as she came to a halt outside her next port of call, fumbling with her electronic key card before disappearing inside. Dolores Gonzalez. Why was she still even working here? She was as old as the hills. Hotel work was physically demanding; he knew that as much as anybody. You were on your feet most of the time. Running around here, there and everywhere. And the shift work could really take it out of you. The hours were so unsociable. And that's before you had to deal with Joe public. Goodness, the things that people found to complain about. The rooms were either too hot, too cold or too noisy. The beds were too hard, too soft or too small. It sometimes felt like he was trapped in a *Goldilocks and the Three Bears* storybook.

He supposed Dolores needed the money. Perhaps she was on her own these days. And she was certainly a long way from home. South America somewhere, he thought. He'd never really taken the time to find out too much detail. He tried not to mix too much with the other staff. As a hotel manager, he obviously had to keep relations professional when there were, inevitably, disciplinary matters to be dealt with. He wasn't there to make friends. Fabian had been the exception, of course. Usually, the only thing that Michael wanted to make was a good impression with anyone higher up the food chain than him.

Dolores just about kept out of trouble as far as he was concerned. She shuffled around the place, her trolley serving as a Zimmer frame as much as anything else. She'd worked at the hotel far longer than he had, but still seemed to be mystified by any technological updates implemented over the years. However, she cleaned the rooms thoroughly. Even if it all took a little longer than expected. And her trips up to the rooms bearing Room Service always resulted in glowing feedback from guests. Such friendly staff, they'd enthuse. Service with a smile, they'd say. Even though Michael suspected that the food had been little more than lukewarm by the time it had arrived.

Imagine the young manager's surprise, therefore, to see the long-serving elderly maid running full pelt out of the room and

10

up the corridor towards him. Her palms were held flat against her cheeks, her eyes wide with horror.

'*Dios mío!*' she shrieked. '*Está muerto!*'

Michael recoiled a little, concerned at the drama of it all. What on earth was up with Dolores? This wasn't very professional at all. He looked around hurriedly, sincerely hoping that they were still alone.

By now, Dolores was tugging on Michael's arm, pulling him in the direction of the room she had just emerged from. 'Come. Come and see,' she urged, weeping.

Michael glanced worriedly over his shoulder as he followed Dolores back to the open doorway. What would the General Manager make of all of this if he turned up now, he fretted? Yet behind him, the lift door remained resolutely closed, the number above it fixed and unmoving.

As he stood outside the room, its door propped open with Dolores' trolley, all Michael could see was darkness. The curtains were still closed and no lights were on.

He was getting a little impatient now. Was this woman frightened of the dark? Had she seen a large spider in the bath? He moved forward to reach for the light switch.

To his amazement, he felt Dolores grabbing his arm, pulling it back. What on earth was going on here?

'Dolores, what is the matter? What's happened? You need to explain or I can't help.'

Dolores removed the hand that was covering her mouth and pointed towards the floor, just beyond the trolley. 'Look! Look! He's dead!' she managed, before dissolving into pitiful sobs.

Michael's eyes had, by now, become accustomed to the dimness of the room in front of him. With both hands resting on the trolley for support, he peered over it guardedly, Dolores' wails ringing in his left ear. He could just make out a figure lying on the floor. A man, by the looks of it, arms thrown outwards, his white sleeves strangely unmatched by the rest of the shirt, dark and obscured in the shadow of the trolley. He was on his back, his head lolled to one side, his face barely visible. Was that a groan he heard? It was hard to tell with all the noise Dolores was making.

11

Instinctively, Michael reached again for the light switch by the door and the room lit up.

'Mr Winterbottom, be careful, what about fingerprints?' Dolores cried.

'What are you talking about, Dolores? Stop being so dramatic. The poor man has probably had a fall. He could have had a heart attack or a seizure, or anything. We need to be able to see what's going on here, so we can help him. I'll call the Emergency Services once I've got a clearer picture. And in the meantime, I've done so many First Aid courses, I've lost count. I might actually be able to do something here.'

Michael was already picturing it now. His photograph in all the hospitality magazines next month; this young Front of House Manager lauded everywhere as a prime example of devotion and dedication to duty. The black-tie awards ceremony at a high-profile hotel in London; accepting his trophy, humbly but with pride, to rapturous applause.

Michael was doing his utmost to recall his best CPR techniques as he moved gingerly around the trolley towards the man whose life he was to save so heroically. He didn't notice the damp carpet, tacky underfoot. He failed to see the pale waxiness of the hand splayed against a wall.

It was only as he leant over the man, debating whether mouth-to-mouth resuscitation was something he really fancied in this day and age, that Michael saw the guest's face. And all the blood. Congealed, widespread, absorbed by the carpet all around the body. Pulling himself abruptly upwards, his face turning slowly ashen, almost rivalling the grey complexion of the figure beneath him, Michael reached out towards the nearby wall for support.

It was extremely fortunate that Dolores Gonzalez had decided to stay close to Michael, tiptoeing into the room behind him. For she was able to break his heavy fall, clasping at his shoulders with all her might, as he fainted backwards into her.

George Henderson, running late after a regional meeting, could hardly believe his eyes as he peered through the open doorway into Room 304, the source of a great deal of noise and commotion. His Front of Desk Manager lay stretched out on his back beside a trolley, his head in the lap of an elderly maid, who was slapping his cheeks between her own intermittent sobs.

'What in heaven's name is going on here? Is Michael alright?' he said, almost gruffly. Nobody answered, of course.

Yet the General Manager's bemusement was soon to be replaced by horror as his bewildered gaze took in the lifeless, blood-stained body of one of his guests lying on the carpet behind the trolley. There seemed to be blood everywhere. And there was no doubt as to the cause of all this carnage. A steak knife had been plunged into the man's chest, its familiar handle still upright, Excalibur-like.

George Henderson's heart sank. The regional meeting had not gone well. It had not gone well at all. Profits were down, but refurbishments were going to have to be paid for. The place was in need of a complete facelift really. And he was under a lot of pressure to drum up more guests somehow or other. This was the last thing he needed. The frenzied killing of a hotel guest was not going to be good for business at all. They were going to have police crawling all over the place, weren't they? It was just a shame that he hadn't been a bit quicker off the mark about getting the security cameras fixed when they'd started playing up. Budget constraints and all that.

George sighed as he tapped at his phone. 'Hello,' he said resignedly, 'I'd like to report a murder.'

Chapter Three

Detective Inspector Sloane drove the short distance from the police station to Lottan Lodge in Lower Haddelton without uttering a word. He kept his eyes on the road, occasionally glancing sideways at his silent companion. Detective Sergeant Thorne stared dolefully out of the passenger window, sighing with great regularity. He appeared to be travelling light, Sloane noted. Thorne's trusty notepad was nowhere to be seen. Things must be bad, the Inspector concluded with a sinking heart.

DI Sloane and DS Thorne had been working together for nearly a year now, an unlikely partnership that seemed to work well. On the one hand, you had the ageing Inspector, a little jaded perhaps, but able to deal with cases with the benefit of hindsight. He'd been doing the job for decades. He'd seen it all before.

And then, on the other, there was the young sergeant, puppy-like in his enthusiasm, diving on cases like a dog with a bone. DS Thorne now knew that, although DI Sloane had a propensity for monologues whilst staring into the middle distance, it was usually worth sticking it out. The Inspector had a knack of getting to the bottom of the matter. His intuition was second-to-none. And DI Sloane had, by now, come to realise that beneath DS Thorne's cheeky-chap banter lay a fierce determination to do his job well. The devil was in the detail, the young sergeant would often say. And he was usually right.

'So, what did she say?' Sloane ventured, as he pulled smoothly into the small hotel car park.

Thorne took a deep breath and stared down at his shoes. 'Not a lot, as it happens. Just that she definitely wants a break. She feels I haven't been putting her first, that I'm not making her a priority.'

'Right. Well, a break isn't the end of the world, is it? That implies it's not for ever.'

'I'm not sure, Sir. Apart from anything else, I don't think she really likes all the shift work I have to do. You know what it's like. She finds it really hard. Especially when I'm having to catch up on my sleep when she wants to go out and do something.' He sighed. 'But I just couldn't imagine myself doing some sort of nine to five desk job, sitting in front of a computer all day. That's just not me. I'm never going to do that. Even for Emily. I'm beginning to wonder if we are actually compatible. Maybe we just want different things.'

'Well, maybe some time apart will help you both work out what you really do want. But I have to agree, Harry, I can't see you doing anything else. You are pretty good at this job. Don't give up on us just yet.'

'Thanks, Sir,' said Thorne, as he pulled his notebook out of his jacket pocket.

Sloane smiled, relieved to see that the status quo had been restored, for now at least.

'Right, let's see what's been going on here. No sign of Forensics yet. Can't see their van anywhere.'

'Well, we can have a chat with a few witnesses in the meantime. It was the General Manager who reported it, but the body was discovered by a maid who'd gone in to clean the room. I don't think they have butlers in these places, do they? Not posh enough. That would make life far too easy though. It's always the butler, isn't it?' Thorne grinned.

Sloane laughed, turning briefly to lock the car, as they headed towards the large glass-fronted reception area of a hotel, where it seemed, to all intents and purposes, to be business as usual. But where, on the third floor, a hotel guest lay drenched in his own blood.

15

Chapter Four

As DS Thorne followed DI Sloane towards the large revolving doors that led into the hotel foyer, he wondered what exactly the etiquette was when it came to getting through them with a senior colleague. Should he bundle in with the Inspector, cosying up behind him, running the risk of being hit by the fast-approaching door behind him, knocking him forwards into his boss? They were on very good terms these days, but did that seem a little over-familiar? Or should he bide his time, wait for a whole new section of his own? Yet would that spoil the moment, ruin the momentum, dilute the overall effect of their arrival, the reassuring sight of these officers who had come to save the day, with one detective nearly half-way across the reception area, while the other pushed in vain at the defiantly unhurried, slowly rotating door he was trapped behind?

The fortuitous arrival of the Forensics team and a couple of police officers in uniform saved DS Thorne from any further debate. With DI Sloane stopping to exchange pleasantries and preliminary thoughts with the pathologist he'd known for years, DS Thorne decided that he would head on inside. He'd look the staff in the eye and pick up on the vibes, he thought. He felt he was quite a good judge of character all in all. Though it was amazing the lies people told. And appearances could be so deceptive. He'd come to the conclusion that people should be considered guilty until proven innocent. And even when innocence had been established, he'd still had his doubts on occasions.

He couldn't wait to start looking at the CCTV too. There must be cameras everywhere in a place like this, he guessed. He loved scouring through CCTV footage. People just didn't realise how much of their lives was being filmed. Was it an invasion of privacy? He didn't really know. But it made his job a whole lot easier, that was for sure. All you had to do was stay on the right side of the law and you'd be alright, he supposed.

16

The mellow jazz that was being piped around the spacious, high-ceilinged reception area seemed a little inappropriate to Thorne. But then, he knew that a bloodied corpse lay somewhere above that high ceiling. Maybe nobody else did. He glanced around him. In actual fact, the place was empty; the low green sofas positioned around low glass tables, with green vases containing dried flowers at their centre, were all unoccupied. Strategically positioned green pendant lighting hung low over the furnishings and the wide reception desk. It was all very green, and very low, Thorne noted.

The only other person present was the young girl standing behind the desk, dressed rather smartly in a white shirt with a fitted, dark waistcoat and a tie. Which was green, of course. With her hair tied up like that, she looked a little like Emily, thought Thorne. Whenever Emily cooked, she always liked to tie her hair back. Said it was unhygienic not to. Did he want hair stew instead of beef, she'd joke? She loved a pun, did Emily. Well, she wouldn't be cooking any stews for him now, would she? He sighed, meeting the eye of the girl politely waiting for him.

'Good morning, how can I help you today?' she asked, smiling. Her eyes were brown, he saw now, not blue like Emily's. But she wasn't bad-looking actually. Not much younger than him, he imagined. He knew that there were boundaries, of course, in this job. Yet there was no harm in looking, he thought. He was a free agent now. Not his choice, but there was nothing he could do about it. Except become a bank clerk or something. He bet this girl would understand what it's like doing shift work. She'd know how you always seemed to be wanting a quick nap, how weekend parties get missed, how you have to watch all your favourite programmes on catch-up. His eyes glanced in the direction of her shiny name badge. Sophie. Nice name. He'd never had a girlfriend called Sophie.

But when Thorne raised his eyes, attempting to grin disarmingly whilst introducing himself, Sophie was no longer looking at him. The light in her warm brown eyes had faded, her smile had faltered, and her gaze was now rigidly set on the black uniforms and high-vis yellow vests outside, not to mention the forensic equipment being unloaded from the white van bearing the words Crime Scene Investigation down the side of it.

17

Not to be outdone, Thorne produced his warrant card, possibly with a slight flourish. She probably hadn't even realised that he was a police officer, he thought, kicking himself. In his grey suit, arriving in an unmarked car, his lanyard was the only real clue to his identity. But then who didn't wear a lanyard these days? Well, at least his tie wasn't green, he thought. Not today, anyway.

'Oh, you're a police officer?' Sophie said, tearing her eyes away from the scene outside.

'Yes. Detective Sergeant Thorne. My colleague, Detective Inspector Sloane, will be in shortly.' Thorne was trying to sound brisk now. He felt a little hurt about the distinct lack of interest. 'We're here to see a Mr George Henderson. Your General Manager, I believe?'

'Yes, yes of course. I'll let him know straightaway.'

Thorne watched with interest as Sophie tentatively picked up the telephone receiver and peered down at the vast array of buttons in front of her. She started to stab, almost randomly, at a number of them, before looking up, with a slightly defeated expression on her face.

'Sorry, I'm fairly new here. I haven't quite got the hang of how the place works yet.' She laughed, embarrassed.

Thorne decided that a smile was in order. The poor girl was probably just a bit confused about what was going on. Maybe a bit scared. Perhaps she had already heard about what had happened. There was no point in denying himself a possible night out with a pretty girl once this case was all wrapped up. There was no harm in keeping his options open for when they'd got to the bottom of this murder.

Unless she'd committed the murder, of course.

The young sergeant prided himself on his gut instinct. It had come up trumps for him on many an occasion. He watched as Sophie's anxious brown eyes nervously took in the arrival of a bustling, frazzled middle-aged man, a green hanky poking neatly out of the top pocket of his expensive suit. The General Manager, he imagined.

'This is Mr Henderson,' she said, smiling politely.

For now, DS Thorne's gut instinct was telling him that this young receptionist was not a callous murderer. Far from it. But then, as he knew, appearances could, indeed, be very deceptive.

Chapter Five

Seated on slightly uncomfortable green bucket chairs in the General Manager's office, DI Sloane and DS Thorne waited patiently as Dolores Gonzalez blew her nose loudly. Very loudly. Sloane glanced briefly at Thorne. As he'd suspected, his sergeant was suppressing a snort of laughter, rubbing at his nose, his head down, all in an attempt to conceal the corners of his mouth that rose so incorrigibly.

The General Manager had bustled off to look into the booking details of the deceased guest. He definitely bustled everywhere, Sloane thought. But maybe that was just today, when one of the paying guests at his hotel lay stabbed to death in a room on the third floor. Sloane had asked Uniform to tape the whole corridor off for now. Anyone staying on that floor would have to be moved to another room with immediate effect. And interviewed at length. Forensics were up there now, doing their bit, examining the body and dusting for prints. He imagined that a hotel room would not be the easiest place to narrow things down, but he knew that David and his team would give it their best shot. He and Thorne would be heading on up shortly, once they'd spoken to a couple of witnesses down here.

With tissues now tucked away, the Inspector decided that it was time to crack on.

'So, Mrs Gonzalez. Is it Mrs Gonzalez? Or Miss?'

'It's Mrs. But you can call me Dolores if you like. Everybody does. I don't mind. It makes me feel a bit younger.' She smiled.

'So, Dolores, I understand that it was you who found the body. I know this is hard, but can you tell us exactly what happened?'

Dolores' body seemed to shrink with horror before their very eyes as she nodded her head slowly. Her black uniform already appeared to hang loosely on her somewhat petite frame. A white apron was tied tightly around her middle, as though to hold her in one piece. She sat rigidly on the office chair that had been set out for her, her delicate legs side by side, her ankles, almost hidden in the black tights she wore, seemingly locked together.

She nervously pushed a loose strand of her grey hair back into position so that it joined the neatly scraped-back bun on her head. As she did so, both detectives noticed the rather large green ring, glittering on her left hand. It had to be green, of course, thought Thorne. Did they even tell the staff what colour jewellery to wear? Surely not? Apart from anything else, he hoped the ring wasn't expensive. You wouldn't want to be dropping something valuable down a guest's toilet, would you?

'Actually, it's hard for me to start,' said Dolores uncertainly. 'Maybe you can ask me some questions, and I can try to answer them?'

'Okay, that's a good idea,' agreed Sloane, not unkindly. 'What time did you enter Room 304?'

'It was around half past ten this morning. I started my shift at ten o'clock and had already been into Room 301 to clean.'

Thorne glanced up from what he was jotting down. 'Is it usual for you to start on the third floor, rather than, say, starting on the first floor and working your way up?'

Sloane raised his eyebrows, quietly impressed. He really didn't miss a trick, his sergeant.

'Officer,' Dolores replied, almost laughing, 'I'm not the only maid here. I don't clean every room in the hotel. There is a whole Housekeeping team.'

Fifteen-love, thought Sloane, as Thorne wrote this all silently down, a nonplussed expression on his face.

'Mr Winterbottom will be able to confirm the time that I went in. He was standing near the lifts just down the corridor. He definitely saw me because he said hello.'

Dolores suddenly looked panicked. 'But he was nowhere near the room. Well, he wasn't that far away. But it definitely wasn't him. I really don't think Mr Winterbottom is a murderer. In my honest opinion, it's more likely that he would be murdered by someone else.'

Sloane watched Dolores' eyes grow wide with alarm at what she had said. 'Of course, no one would really murder him,' she gushed, clearly trying to make amends. 'Please forget I said that. It was a silly joke. There are no murderers at Lottan Lodge.'

'Well, apart from the person who stabbed your guest in Room 304 to death.' Thorne added, somewhat patronisingly.

21

Was that fifteen-all, wondered Sloane?

'We will be speaking to Mr Winterbottom in due course. I believe he is currently being taken care of by a First Aid Officer.'

Dolores' hands flew to her face. 'Is he alright? I managed to catch him as he fell. Break his fall, I think you say? It was such a shock for both of us, seeing all that blood, that poor man lying there.'

'Mr Winterbottom is absolutely fine. He's having a lie-down and a cup of tea. I can imagine it was all a bit frightening for you both.' Sloane smiled.

'Your English is excellent, Dolores, though I can't quite place your accent? Where are you originally from, if you don't mind me asking?'

'Of course not. I'm from Colombia.' She cast her eyes in the direction of Thorne's notepad. 'It's spelt with an 'o', not a 'u',' she said.

Sloane couldn't help but grin. It was definitely thirty-fifteen now.

'I've been over here an awfully long time now. We came over to London because of my late husband's job. We took a while to settle in, but by the time he passed away, I had made England my home.'

'I'm sorry for your loss,' said Sloane sombrely, his own grief surfacing momentarily. It never really went away if he was honest, and Helen had been dead for over thirty years now.

'He died a long time ago now. But thank you, that's very kind of you.' The Inspector sensed in Dolores a kindred spirit, a lost soul, never quite able to escape the shadow of grief.

'I go home to Bogotá when I can, though it doesn't tend to be that often. I have to do lots of saving. I actually come from a very small village outside Bogotá. The countryside is very pretty around there. As it is in many places. Colombia is such a beautiful country, you know. We only moved to the city to find work.' Dolores looked uncertainly at the two detectives. 'I know exactly what you are thinking of right now. Especially as you are policemen. But, as a matter of fact, we are just as famous for our coffee and our orchids. And, of course, our emeralds.' She briefly waved the deep-green gemstone on her ring finger.

'This was a gift from my late husband. I never take it off.'

Sloane nodded understandingly. Thorne was thinking of the guests' toilets.

'Getting back to the murdered guest,' said Thorne, 'Did you notice anything suspicious or untoward when you entered the room earlier today? Apart from the body on the floor, of course.'

'Well, it was pretty dark in there. It was only because my trolley ran into something on the floor and wouldn't budge that I looked down. That's when I saw him.'

'So, you pushed your trolley right into the room? That seems a little strange. Isn't it more usual to leave it outside on the corridor?' Thorne tilted his head, adopting a distinctly quizzical expression.

Sloane had forgotten the score line by now, but he could see that Thorne wasn't going down without a fight.

'Yes, it is. But my hip has been giving me quite a few problems recently. It's so much easier for me to have everything in the room with me when I'm cleaning. I'm no spring chicken, officer.'

'Of course. Now, obviously we will have to confirm the identity of victim. But, for the moment, can I ask if the guest in Room 304 was known to you?'

'I don't think so. I didn't really get a good look at him though. As soon as I saw all the blood, I ran to get help. It was all such a shock. I'm still feeling a little shaky now if I am honest.'

Dolores turned her head nervously as the office door opened abruptly and the General Manager rushed into the room.

'Okay' he said, 'I've got some details on the dead man upstairs. He was booked in under the name of Mr Smith. He's been coming here for the odd night for about six or seven months now. Always paid with cash.'

Thorne snorted. Even Sloane rolled his eyes.

George Henderson nodded. 'Yes, possibly an alias, I know. Maybe a bit of subterfuge has been going on, who's to say? But he might have stuck to his actual first name with any luck. It's Anthony.'

23

Chapter Six

Sophie watched discreetly as Dolores Gonzalez emerged from the General Manager's office, skirting out of the way of Michael Winterbottom as she did so. Michael was nervously rubbing his sweaty palms on the front of his jacket as he headed in. So, it was his turn now, was it? Let's hope they gave him a taste of his own medicine. He was so pompous, so judgemental. So slimy.

Fabian had warned her, of course. He'd told her to keep her distance as much as she could. But that was easier said than done. He was always there, breathing down her neck, telling her what she'd done wrong. As if she wasn't on edge already. She'd been dying to compare notes with Fabian, fill him in on it all. But she hadn't been able to get hold of him. Where the hell was he, she wondered? He seemed to have disappeared off the face of the earth.

She knew that it wouldn't be long until she was hauled in by those two detectives. She would have to think very carefully about what she was going to say. She'd managed to get through the job interview without arousing suspicion. Even though she could tell that Michael didn't like her at all. He obviously didn't think she was suited to the job. But she knew that they were desperate with Fabian leaving like he did. She supposed she had to give dear Mr Winterbottom some credit. He was quite right. Why the hell would she take on a job in this boring old hotel unless she had a very good reason to?

Chapter Seven

'Take a seat, Mr Winterbottom,' said DI Sloane, gesturing to the small wooden chair that had supported Dolores Gonzalez well enough, but that now appeared wholly inadequate. The Inspector watched as the slim, long limbs of this pale young man folded awkwardly into position. The stick insects that he had kept as a child sprung to mind. Elongated masters of camouflage, escaping detection by blending into the surrounding vegetation. He had already noted the green tie, which seemed to be de rigueur here, but now he spotted the green socks, an almost perfect match with the carpet beneath them. He remembered, too, that stick insects were nocturnal, with the females tending to mainly eat during their waking hours. The males preferred to spend their nights searching for a mate. Still, Sloane thought, being nocturnal would certainly help if night shifts were part of your job. As far as his twig-like pets were concerned, he had eventually decided to move onto goldfish. Once he'd seen how they moulted and ate their own leftover skin.

'Thank you for coming to speak to us, Mr Winterbottom,' began Sloane.

'Firstly, can you talk us through what you saw, and why you were up on the third floor earlier this morning?'

'Well,' replied Michael, taking a deep breath, 'I was about to do some room inspections with Mr Henderson, the General Manager, who was here a moment ago. I'm the Front of Desk Manager.'

Sloane wondered if he was supposed to be impressed.

'What exactly does your job entail, Mr Winterbottom?'

'Well, let's just say that if this was some sort of grand house, a stately pile somewhere out in the countryside, I would be the butler.'

There was a brief silence. Sloane didn't have to glance sideways to know that Thorne's pen hovered temporarily over his notepad, and his bowed head concealed a grin.

But then his sergeant looked up. He clearly couldn't help himself. 'Perhaps we should arrest you now, Mr Winterbottom. It's always the butler, isn't it?'

Yet, while the two detectives smiled, clearly amused, Michael Winterbottom stared at them in horror.

'I had nothing to do with Anthony Smith's death. Why on earth would I kill one of our hotel guests? It was Dolores who dragged me up to that room. I was as shocked as she was.'

'Of course, Mr Winterbottom. And I do apologise for my sergeant's sense of humour. I realise that this is a distressing time for everybody here at Lottan Lodge.'

Michael nodded, but the defensive, nervous look in his eyes remained. He wiped his palms on his thighs.

'Yes, I'm sorry, Mr Winterbottom,' added Thorne. 'However, can I just check something? The name of the victim hasn't been released yet. Mr Henderson passed on that information to us before you entered the room. Apart from coming across his dead body earlier today, exactly what contact have you had with the man lying dead in Room 304?'

Chapter Eight

DI Sloane glanced only briefly at his reflection in the lift mirror, his eyes drawn instead to his colleague next to him, head craned upwards, turning on his heels, backwards and forwards, his eyes alert and searching.

'What are you looking for, Thorne? Are you thinking we have a suspect hiding in the lift shaft, clinging on to the lift roof above us or something?' Sloane smiled.

'I'm looking for cameras, Sir. A hotel like this should have them here, there and everywhere. With any luck, we'll be able to see exactly who came up to the third floor these last few hours.'

'Good thinking. We'll check with the Hotel Manager when we go back down again.'

'Yes. This could really be an open and shut case. Excuse the pun.' Thorne grinned.

Famous last words, thought Sloane. But he couldn't help but smile too as the lift doors opened onto the third floor.

The Inspector was pleased to see the cordons in place, and the uniformed officer in position at the start of the corridor.

'They're just up there, Sir,' the policeman indicated, pointing to where the Forensics team stood packing up their metal cases.

Thorne was on the other side of the police tape before the Inspector had even begun to contemplate whether he would go over or under it.

'Want a hand, Sir?' Thorne asked, offering his arm.

'I hope that's a joke,' said Sloane, as he clambered over the cordon. If he was honest, he did have to watch his back these days.

'Inspector, hello again,' said one of the pathologists, pulling down the hood of his white overalls and removing his paper mask.

'What have you got for us then, David?' asked Sloane, peering briefly through the open doorway.

'Well, the victim is a white male, aged around forty. He appears to have been stabbed twice. Once in the abdomen, and once in the heart. And that's where the murder weapon was left. In his heart. The blade used to kill him looks like a steak knife. We'll be able to confirm with the kitchen staff if it belongs to the hotel.

The man was fully dressed and the bed was still made up. This would fit in with our estimate for the time of death. He clearly wasn't killed this morning. Fully established rigor mortis is still evident. The body is cold and stiff. So, our victim has definitely been dead for longer than nine hours. Also, as you probably know by now, if death had occurred more than sixteen hours ago, rigor mortis would be starting to wear off. I would say that this murder took place yesterday evening, sometime after six o'clock.'

'Great. That's very interesting. Anything else in the room of interest?'

'Yes, I would say so. There are two phone chargers, but no mobile phones anywhere in sight. There is also no wallet, or any form of ID in there. In fact, this man was travelling very light. He did have a toothbrush with him, so we've taken swabs for DNA checks. Obviously, if he's not on the database, that's not going to get us very far. As always, we've brushed everything we can for fingerprints and we'll take fingerprints from any relevant staff, particularly those who were working yesterday evening.

There is a small bunch of flowers and an unopened box of chocolates on the bed. Maybe not that surprising as it was Valentine's Day. What is interesting is that there is also an envelope containing a wad of £20 notes, totalling £200. The name Anthony is written in capitals on the front of the envelope. So, I'm guessing that's a good place to start in terms of the victim's identity, as well as anything the hotel has on their system.'

'I really don't think this was a robbery,' continued the pathologist. 'Why leave all that cash behind? And why take the phones, but not the chargers, just sitting there plugged in, presumably charging the phones at the time? Given the date, the Valentine's gifts, and the fact that the blade was left sitting in the man's heart, I'm inclined to think that this murder may well have something to do with affairs of the heart. Though what that envelope stuffed with money has got to do with it all, I really don't know. I guess that's where you two come in.'

28

Chapter Nine

'Penny for your thoughts?' asked Sloane, as he drove slowly back towards the station.

Thorne was gazing silently out of the window beside him. 'Actually, I was thinking that Emily would probably have stabbed me if I'd bought her those cheap flowers and that very basic box of chocolates for Valentine's Day. There was literally a clearance price on the flowers, and those chocolates are on offer everywhere at the moment.'

'Yes, but is it enough of a reason to kill the man? Wouldn't it have been easier just to dump him?'

Even as the words left his mouth, Sloane realised what he'd said.

'Sorry, I didn't mean that.' He grimaced.

'I know. Don't worry. And just for the record, I'd been planning on buying Emily something a little bit more special than that.' He sighed. 'Something a bit more sparkly, let's just say.'

'What? A ring?'

'Yes. Can you believe it? Talk about being at crossed purposes. There's me planning to get down on one knee, while she's deciding to run for the hills.' He shook his head despairingly. 'Well, I suppose I've saved myself a few bob for now.'

He sighed again. 'As for that hotel's CCTV being on the blink. What a joke. And the staff don't seem to know if they're coming or they're going. The hotel manager doesn't appear to have his eye on the ball at all, the maid thought she was there for a cosy chat rather than to help us with our enquiries, and that young manager was a bit shifty. I get that it's his business to remember guests' names, but there was still something distinctly dodgy about him. The only person I spoke to with any modicum of trustworthiness or common sense was that girl on reception, Sophie. In fact, we definitely need to go back and interview her formally. She may well be able to join a few dots for us.'

29

'Well, let's see what Forensics come back with. And hopefully before too long, someone out there will realise that 'Anthony Smith' has disappeared without trace. Worst part of the job, of course, informing an unsuspecting soul that their loved one is no longer with us. I'm not looking forward to that, I have to say.'

'Yeah, I know what you mean. But call me a cynic, I'll be watching that person very carefully. An awful lot of murders are carried out by someone known to the victim. You know as well as I do that there's a good chance that whoever eventually claims back this dead man is the person who killed him in the first place.'

Chapter Ten

Bernardo Castillo stood at the window of his hotel room, looking up at the night sky. It was free of cloud that night and dappled with shimmering stars, as though glitter had been sprinkled across the vast, velvety darkness high above. The moon's ethereal glow beamed down upon the world below, lighting the ripples on the river outside, now twinkling joyously.

But Bernardo saw none of this. He took nothing in. He didn't think back to the glorious summer evenings that he'd spent as a child at home in Spain, his head tilted backwards, his eyes fixed on the glistening galaxies high above him. His grandmother had once told him that wishing on shooting stars could bring true love into your life. He'd always been on the look-out for them after that. Imagine Bernardo's dismay, and bitter disappointment, the day he'd discovered that these magical sources of romance were nothing more than meteors, mere bits of rock, burning up in the earth's atmosphere. What a let-down, he'd thought, but it explained a lot.

Bernardo had actually had a slightly better view up until the previous night, when he was still on the third floor. But they'd moved him down here to the second floor today, since they'd found the body. Anthony's body.

And, of course, he wasn't here for the views.

The police were due to be interviewing him the following day and he'd been busy rehearsing his lines. It was what he did for a living after all; learning lines, playing a part, pretending to be someone he wasn't. He was literally an actor. So, there shouldn't be any problem, should there?

Yet, there was a lot more at stake here, wasn't there? If he wasn't overly convincing, this wasn't just a question of some feeble applause or bad reviews. Bernardo wondered what happened if you omitted facts, said as little as possible, left it to the police to do all the digging? They didn't always get there, did they? If certain things came to light, he imagined that he could always claim a touch of memory loss. Though at the grand old age of forty, that probably wouldn't ring particularly true, he guessed.

Bernardo sighed and sat down slowly on the edge of the large bed, his hands resting either side of him. When he looked across at the dressing-table mirror, he could still see traces of his stage make-up. He cut a solitary figure, alone in that dark, silent room. Away from the stage lights and the audience, who even was he? He wasn't sure that he knew anymore. He barely recognised the unsmiling eyes and furrowed brow reflecting back at him.

And even as he finally drifted into sleep sometime later, lying, still dressed, on top of the bed covers, a deep frown remained etched on Bernardo's forehead, visible in the silver light that streamed down on him from the hazy moon crossing the sky outside.

Chapter Eleven

February 17

DS Thorne was staring at a computer in the police station office when DI Sloane took the call. Thorne was meant to be on a mission. He really hadn't taken to Michael Winterbottom, or Dolores Gonzalez. If either of them had slipped up somewhere along the line, or had something to hide, he was planning to find out. If only he could stop thinking about Emily.

'Right,' said Sloane, 'We've had someone report a missing person. A woman has phoned in to say her husband has disappeared without explanation. A male going by the name of Anthony Pritchard.'

'Sounds like it's our mystery man from Room 304,' said Thorne, tearing his forlorn gaze away from his computer screen; a blank screen that bore testament to a couple of hours of half-hearted research, interspersed with all too frequent bouts of regret, pain, and bewilderment.

'Yes, I suppose she's waited a couple of days to be sure, who knows?'

'Yeah, I don't know how long I would've waited if Emily had gone missing. Ten minutes, maybe. Still, it wouldn't be my problem now, would it?'

'Do you want to come with me to do this?' suggested Sloane. 'We need to keep you busy, I think. You know, there's always someone worse off than you, and today it's this poor woman.'

'Sorry, Sir. I know I keep harping on about my failed love life. But, yes, I definitely want to come with you, if that's okay.'

'Right. No time like the present. I've got her address. She lives out in Newtown Park, about twenty minutes or so away. You can fill me in on anything you've come across so far. Forensics seemed to have drawn a blank.'

Grabbing his jacket and following DI Sloane down the stairs to the car, Thorne smiled feebly. 'You know me, Sir, I leave no stone unturned. Well, usually. And you're right, it is taking my mind off things. Sort of.'

'What did you think of that actor?' asked Sloane. 'He seemed a bit nervous. It was probably a bit of a shock for him to find that he was the only other hotel guest booked in along that third-floor corridor on the night of the murder. Though he does have a very credible reason for staying at the hotel itself, being in the show at the theatre in Lower Haddelton. I'd actually been thinking of going to see it myself, funnily enough.'

'I've never heard of him though. I don't think he's particularly famous. You'd never know he was Spanish, would you? Apart from his Latin looks obviously. And his name.' Thorne laughed. 'He does seem to have lost any trace of an accent though. I suppose he's lived most of his life over here. What was he, fourteen when he came over?'

Sloane nodded.

'Anyway,' continued Thorne, 'I don't think he had anything to do with the murder. But you never know. Obviously, it's hard to find connections to the victim at this stage, when we don't really know who our victim is.'

'What about the receptionist we spoke to yesterday, Sophie Hawkins? She was quite a cool customer,' said Sloane

'I thought she was very pleasant, very professional,' said Thorne. 'I guess she doesn't have anything to hide. Though she was on duty the evening of the murder, just like Michael Winterbottom and Dolores Gonzalez. Not that I won't do a bit of digging about Sophie, naturally. Find out a bit more about her. For professional reasons entirely, of course.' He laughed, glancing out of the window. The houses were losing their grandeur now, the cars parked outside them less shiny.

'Right. We're nearly there now,' said Sloane. 'I'll lead this. Maybe leave your notebook in your pocket for this one. It's going to be tough for this poor woman. Not only is her husband dead, if we've got the right man, but he was found murdered in a hotel on Valentine's Day, booked in under an alias.'

'Absolutely, Sir. I get that it's not going to be easy to fill her in on all of this. However, I will be watching her very carefully. For all we know, this woman realised that something was going on, and we have the perfect motive for murder.'

Chapter Twelve

Finding somewhere to park near to Anthony Pritchard's house had proved to be something of a challenge for DI Sloane and DS Thorne. The customers of the small garage at the end of the road clearly monopolised any available parking space. Vehicles awaiting MOTs or new batteries lined the small residential street, and an unoccupied spot between the garage's pick-up truck and a badly dented van had turned out to be their only option.

DI Sloane pushed his wing mirror in carefully as he looked across at the front door that they were about to knock on, at the home that they were about to bring to its knees, the family life that they were about to devastate. His stomach lurched. He had been given plenty of training in this sort of thing, and it certainly wasn't the first time he had been involved in this type of scenario. But it never got any easier.

He could hear Thorne clearing his throat, and was aware of him pulling down his shoulders, raised with tension, as they negotiated their way around the small red sports car on the driveway, a little battered, its soft-top barely intact, but still classically beautiful. Two large Victorian stone cast urns flanked the plastic front door. The ornate pots, with the acanthus leaf motif that ran up them, were currently empty, but Sloane still found them impressive nevertheless. He rang the bell.

The door was opened almost immediately. A young woman put her finger to her lips.

'Do come in. Thank you for coming round so quickly,' she almost mouthed. 'Sorry, my little boy is having an afternoon nap. I'd tried to get to the door when I saw you coming up the driveway. He gets so grouchy if he doesn't have a bit of a sleep in the day. I didn't want the doorbell to wake him up. Would it be okay if we whispered, at least until we get into the living room?'

Sloane nodded silently as he wiped his feet. 'Would you like us to take our shoes off?' he asked. He pointed at his feet to make sure she understood, as he was speaking so quietly.

'Goodness, no. Definitely not. Come on in.'

The house was one of a row of 1930s semi-detached properties, all possibly in need of a lick of paint or maybe new windows. The road wasn't exactly run-down. Just full of suburban, pebble-dashed housing stock that was due a touch of updating. In keeping with its surroundings, there had appeared to be nothing remotely remarkable about Anthony Pritchard's house; nothing that would prepare the two detectives for what they would encounter inside.

It was really only when the two detectives followed the young woman into the living room, knocked through to create one large room, that their eyes widened. In fact, they were both stopped in their tracks.

'Do take a seat,' the woman said, still whispering, even after quietly closing the living room door behind them.

Sloane loved antiques. He loved nothing more than strolling around antique markets and shops when he had a free afternoon. He'd even been to a few auctions. He couldn't really afford much of the furniture he'd read up on, but he could still appreciate it. And he had invested in the odd chair or desk. But, my goodness, he thought, the furniture in this room was something else. In his searches, he'd seen examples of everything from Georgian and Regency times, right through to the Victorian and Edwardian periods; he knew his mahogany from his walnut; he'd admired brass castors, cabriole legs, and claw and ball feet. And he was certainly acquainted with the Baroque style, with its elaborate, decorative details, and its strong and dramatic curves. The sofa that the young woman was gesturing towards was upholstered in a sumptuous damask fabric and edged with gilded carved mouldings, all flowers and cherubs amongst scrolls of foliage; its legs were carved from solid mahogany. The sofa had seen better days, admittedly, but Sloane knew that it was the real deal, and worth a fortune.

A chandelier, designed for significantly higher ceilings, hung low over the centre of the room, its hand-cut, opaque crystals strung together in chains, casting an incongruous, iridescent light out on the proceedings below. Sloane had the good sense to duck as he headed towards the majestic sofa, so out of place next to the small double-glazed windows that lined the front of the house. Judging by the jangling behind him, he guessed that Thorne hadn't quite thought it through.

Once seated, the Inspector had a few moments to take it all in; the large gilded mirror, tarnished but magnificent, clashing wildly with the 1970s York Stone fireplace; the oval mahogany dining table and ornate chairs at the other end of the room, slightly battered but extremely elegant nonetheless; the chaise longue, upholstered in a faded, luxurious floral fabric, squeezed in beside them along the wall; the Georgian writing desk, with its intricately carved legs, against another wall; the substantial satinwood bureau with its club feet and the decorative engravings in the bookcase that sat above it, lined with rows of identical leather bound books; and finally the rather grand Ottoman foot stool, perhaps losing a little of its horsehair stuffing, that this unsuspecting young woman now took her place upon.

She was somewhat younger than he had expected. Forensics had confirmed that 'Mr Smith' was around the age of forty. This lady appeared to be in her mid-twenties at the most. But maybe she just had youthful looks. She wore her long brown hair loose, with just a simple band across the top of her head to hold it back. With her pale skin, free of any make-up, and an aquiline nose, hers was the kind of beauty that crept up on you; not immediately evident, but once you saw it, you found it hard to believe that you had ever missed it in the first place. Sloane allowed his gaze to take the rest of her in. She appeared to be slight in build, but the long, tiered dress that she wore made it difficult to tell. It swamped her really. There was something distinctly delicate about this young woman, he felt, as he watched her wrap her arms around herself in an act of unconscious self-comfort perhaps; her quilted gilet and sagging woollen socks, as much of a mis-match with her pretty paisley dress as the furniture was with the house, were to be wholly inadequate in providing the warmth and protection she now needed.

The Inspector glanced briefly at the framed photographs on the mantelpiece. One of them, in black and white, was a beautifully captured moment of a young family, a close-up of three smiling faces. Sloane had seen the dead man for himself; slim, dark-haired, probably very attractive before all the stabbing took place. His heart sank.

The young woman addressed them, still whispering. 'So, I think I explained to a colleague of yours that Anthony seems to have gone missing. I waited a couple of days because he does come and go quite a lot. Because of his job. But he was due home on the fifteenth.'

She glanced at the large vase of red roses at the centre of her beautiful wooden table.

'We had Valentine's Day apart, but he'd said he was planning a lovely treat to make up for it. He's very romantic.' She laughed shyly.

'Anyway, there's been no sign of him, and I can't get hold of him on his mobile. He can be difficult to contact at times, to tell you the truth. He's so busy with his job. In fact, I'm half worried he's going to walk through the door while you're here, and I'm going to be arrested for wasting police time.' She laughed again, a little nervously.

'So, how do we do this? Do I give you a description? A couple of photos?'

Sloane took a deep breath. Thorne adjusted his shirtsleeves.

But the sound of a child crying distracted the young mother, and she jumped up, shrugging. 'Sorry, I'll just go and get him,' she said. She was still speaking very quietly. Force of habit, Sloane supposed.

The two detectives sat in silence as they waited. Sloane stared curiously at a large oil painting, a portrait from times gone by, in a heavy gilt frame at the far end of the room. It was enormous, far larger than the television on the wall near to where they sat. Sloane, almost nodding with approval, barely noticed the young woman come back into the room.

'Say hello to these nice policemen,' she said. Her voice seemed strangely loud after all the whispering. She smiled down at the small, dark-haired child that she was carrying on her hip, before turning back to Sloane and Thorne. 'This is Henry. And I don't think I've introduced myself properly yet. I'm Arabella.'

Chapter Thirteen

Bernardo smiled weakly as he opened the door of his room to Michael Winterbottom.

'Some lunch and a pot of tea,' announced the young manager, holding a tray out in front of him.

'But I didn't order anything,' said Bernardo.

'Compliments of the house, Mr Castillo. You've been inconvenienced somewhat, having to move rooms like this. And I'm sure it's all been a nasty shock, hearing about what's happened. Shall I bring your lunch in?'

'Thank you. That's very kind of you. This is the second time you've gone to all this trouble. I'm very grateful.'

'You're not vegetarian or anything, are you? Sorry, I hadn't checked.'

'No, I'm Spanish. So quite partial to a bit of ham myself. Not that they're mutually exclusive, of course. Being Spanish and vegetarian.' He laughed.

'I've always wanted to go to Spain,' said Michael, a little dreamily. 'Which part are you from?'

'I'm from Andalusia in the south. I was born in Granada, which is beautiful, though for some reason, my parents thought it was a good idea to move over to London when I was still quite young. They thought there would be more opportunity for them, and for me.'

'They must have been mad, leaving behind all that sunshine,' Michael laughed, glancing pointedly at the leaden sky outside Bernardo's window.

'I know. I'm half-thinking about going back, setting up a little bed and breakfast place near the coast. It's so gorgeous there, particularly if you get off the beaten track.'

'Wouldn't you miss the acting though?'

'Oh, you know I'm an actor?'

Michael blushed. 'Only because I walk past the theatre to get here and I saw your name on the posters. You've got quite a distinctive name, obviously.'

'Yes.' Bernardo hesitated. 'Actually, I wanted to ask you something. A little favour. You don't have to do it if you feel uncomfortable about it, of course.'

'I'm here to help if I can,' offered Michael, delighted to be involved in the intricacies of this handsome Spanish man's life. He was probably a little older than him, maybe about forty, but Mr Castillo seemed to have lost none of the allure that these Latin men are fortunate enough to be born with. Certainly in Michael's eyes anyway.

'The thing is, you know that you also kindly brought me up some supper on the evening of Valentine's Day, the night of the murder? Well, let me put it this way, I haven't mentioned to the police that I was on the premises at the time. I think they are still assuming that I was on stage while that man was being stabbed to death. They obviously know that I am appearing in the play for these three weeks.'

Michael caught Bernardo's eye and held it, just for a second.

'So, basically, me bringing you up that supper never happened?'

Bernardo nodded.

'Mr Castillo, rest assured, your secret is safe with me. The police only asked me if I had brought any food up to Room 304. Which I hadn't. And don't worry about the kitchen staff, they're clueless at the best of times. Funnily enough, it was me that decided you needed a bit of supper and I dealt with it personally. You'd have been waiting all night if I'd given it to the only other person on duty. She's a bit slow, to say the least.'

'Thank you, Mr Winterbottom. *Gracias.* I really appreciate this. If there's ever anything I can do in return, do let me know.'

'*De nada,* Mr Castillo, *de nada.* Enjoy your lunch.'

Michael Winterbottom smiled as he turned to leave. He was still smiling when he reached the lift at the end of the corridor, where the red light on the camera blinked, as it did from time to time.

Chapter Fourteen

'Can I get you gentlemen a cup of tea or something?' Arabella asked, as she placed her young son on the well-worn polyester carpet and handed him a couple of toys covered in brightly-coloured buttons and lights.

'No, don't go to any trouble,' replied Sloane. 'If you don't mind taking a seat again, we need to run through a few things with you.'

'Of course. I'm sure you are very busy men. Lots of criminals to catch and all that.'

'Mrs Pritchard, when did you last see your husband?'

'Right, well, it's actually Mrs Pritchard-to-be, by the way.'

She waved her hand at them, showing off the neat solitaire diamond on her ring finger. Sloane didn't know who to feel more sorry for; this poor woman, or Thorne, with his own thwarted romantic dreams.

'And it's Winthorpe-Holmes, my surname. Bit of a mouthful, I know. Frankly, I can't wait to lose it. Arabella Pritchard sounds so much better. But do call me Arabella.'

Sloane moved slightly, adjusting his position. Thorne looked down at his feet.

'Anyway, the last time I saw Anthony was on the eighth of February.'

'The eighth of February?' said Sloane. 'That's quite some time ago.'

'Yes, I know. Anthony travels a lot for work. I should say that I have actually spoken to him since the eighth. But he's been away for work since then. The last time I spoke to him was on the fourteenth. It was Valentine's Day, of course. He'd sent me some beautiful roses, which had arrived first thing, and he phoned around lunchtime to say hello. He seemed his usual, cheerful self really. He did say he was missing me and that he couldn't wait to see me the next day.'

Sloane watched as Arabella's eyes suddenly glistened, and she glanced down towards her young son.

'Arabella, can you confirm Anthony's age? Have you got a photo of him to hand?'

'He's forty, nearly forty-one. That's him up there.' Arabella pointed to the mantelpiece. 'But I can send you a couple of photos of him alone, if you want. Will you make some kind of on-line appeal?'

'The thing is… I'm sorry to have to say this… But a body has been found in a hotel room in Lower Haddelton. We haven't managed to identify the victim as yet, but he was checked in as Anthony Smith. And his appearance and age seem to match your partner's.' Sloane hated using that word. It sounded so business-like. But what could he say? Boyfriend? Lover? Fiancé? They all sounded a bit inappropriate, especially in these awful circumstances.

'A hotel in Lower Haddelton? That's only twenty minutes away. I can see no reason why Anthony would stay somewhere so close to home. And Smith could be this poor man's real surname, you know? It's highly probable, in fact. Why would somebody check themselves into a hotel under a false name?'

Sloane could see pain and uncertainty vying with the indignation and disbelief in Arabella's eyes.

'Officers, can I ask, have you seen the body of this man yourselves? Did he really look anything like Anthony?' She grabbed the photograph from the mantelpiece and thrust it towards the anguished detectives.

'Forensic tests are going to provide further clarification, of course. But we would ask that you come in to identify the body, if only to tell us that it definitely isn't him.'

'Absolutely. I really don't think it is him. I just can't believe that Anthony would be in a nearby hotel on Valentine's Day. It doesn't make sense. He'd said he was in Norwich.'

'Have you tried calling his office?'

'No. He said they were very strict about personal phone calls. And he is usually out and about anyway. He travels all over the country for his job. I always leave him a message on his mobile and he calls me back as soon as he can.'

Even as she spoke, Sloane could see the doubt etched all over the young woman's face.

'What about his social media accounts? Have you checked any of those?'

'Oh, he hates all that. Says it's just a load of showing off. He's not on anything.'

'Arabella, do you have someone that can be with you? This must all be a bit of a shock.'

'Yes, I'll call my neighbour over the road. She's at home with a little one too.'

'Right. So, here is my card. If you could email me the photos of Anthony. I wondered whether we could also take a toothbrush or comb? Something to give us a DNA comparison?'

Sloane and Thorne exchanged silent glances as Arabella quietly swept up her son and left the room.

Still intrigued by all the surrounding grandeur, Sloane was now regretting the absence of Thorne's ever-present notepad. What had Arabella said her surname was? There was definitely a bit of a story behind all this. Something didn't quite add up.

'Did you get her surname?' he whispered as they headed out to the hall. Thorne nodded.

They watched as Arabella came resignedly down the stairs. 'Here you go. It's Anthony's toothbrush. But I'll be blaming you when he gets home and moans that it's missing.' She tried to laugh. But her eyes were beseeching, willing these two detectives to play along.

'Yes, you can say it's all my fault. Anthony can have a new toothbrush on me if he needs one.' DI Sloane was not a man who was short on empathy.

'Thank you, Inspector. I'll call you if he gets home.'

Call it a sixth sense, but, even with his back to her, Sloane could tell that Arabella was watching them until they disappeared behind the dented van.

'That was tough,' he said, as he pulled out his wing-mirror and got into the car.

But Thorne wasn't listening. With his head tilted forwards over his phone, he was engrossed in a message.

'Oh my God,' he said, as he threw himself into the passenger seat, 'You are not going to believe this. The station has just received another call about a missing person. A woman whose husband is missing.'

'Not another one? They're falling like flies out there. Perhaps it's the Valentine's Day effect?'

'But here's the thing. The woman's name is Sarah apparently. Sarah Johnson. And the name of her missing husband is Anthony. Anthony Pritchard.'

Chapter Fifteen

February 18

Dolores Gonzalez leant into the large storage cupboard that sat tucked away at the end of the first-floor corridor. She hummed to herself as she rearranged the pristine white towels and fresh linen. Using agency staff over the Christmas and New Year period, when things had been a little busier, had been all well and good, but now that it was quieter, it was up to the regulars like her to pick up the pieces and sort everything out again. From time to time, she tutted at the disarray before her. It felt like she was having to fold and smooth everything she came across.

Dolores had always taken pride in her work at Lottan Lodge. If a job is worth doing, it is worth doing well, she would always say to anyone who would listen. But after nearly twenty years here, she was starting to feel that she had done her bit. She'd worked very hard for this hotel. She'd given it her all, really. She'd done the shifts that nobody else wanted to do; she'd covered when people were sick; she'd been unfailingly polite to the guests; she'd tolerated difficult colleagues. It had become her life, really. When she lost Juan all those years ago, her work here had become a welcome distraction. What else was she going to do in the evenings but help out in the hotel restaurant or take up food orders to rooms? If the truth be told, she quite enjoyed getting to know the guests. She loved the cosy little chats that invariably happened when she appeared with a tray, its silver dome bearing such promise. And she always greeted returning customers with genuine warmth. She would always recognise them. Dolores never forgot a face.

Whenever Michael took her to one side for a quiet word, she would always tell him that public relations were very important in the hospitality sector. Honestly, what did that young whippersnapper know, she'd think? She loved that word. She'd only discovered it after she'd met Michael Winterbottom.

Dolores had been on the verge of leaving on several occasions now. Years of scrimping and saving meant that she certainly no longer needed to work. But, for one reason or another, she wasn't ready to leave Lottan Lodge quite yet. Retirement was a daunting prospect for someone like Dolores. She liked to keep busy, and she loved being around people. Any family that she still had were back in Colombia. Deep down, she was very scared of being lonely; of turning into one of those pitiful pensioners who lured unsuspecting victims, shop workers or fellow bus passengers, into lengthy conversations about the price of bread or the recent unseasonal weather. She certainly couldn't see herself playing Bridge, and there were only so many Zumba classes that she'd want to go to.

As Dolores took a step backwards, straightening up and rubbing her back, she could swear that she heard the sound of light footsteps behind her. She stood very still. Was she imagining it, or could she feel hot breath on her neck? Out of the corner of her eye, she glanced in the direction of the lift. The long, dimly-lit corridor was deserted. Her shadow stretched vaguely across the dark patterned carpet. Looming there too, she noticed, was the shadow of another, taller figure, caught in the wall-light behind them. For once in her life, Dolores found herself hoping that Michael was checking up on her, making sure that the towels and sheets were all in perfect order, and that she was going to close the cupboard doors properly. Whether the state of this storage cupboard actually had anything to do with him was debatable, of course. He did seem to think that he was running the show at times. He poked his nose into everything, whenever he could. And George Henderson didn't seem to mind at all. In fact, Dolores thought that the General Manager seemed quite grateful.

Yet, as she slowly looked over her shoulder, it was not the Front of Desk Manager who stood there, hands on his hips, poised to admonish. Instead, it was Sophie, the new receptionist who waited there, wide-eyed, clutching a selection of knives and forks. Mainly knives, Dolores noted.

'Can I help you?' Dolores asked. The girl seemed very nervous, she thought.

'I'm so sorry. I think I've got a bit lost. Michael asked me to put some bits and pieces back into the storage cupboard.'

'Cutlery is all stored on the ground floor. The cupboard you need is directly below this one.'

'Goodness, yes of course. Thank you. I think I must have been thinking of the American system. The first floor is the ground floor over there.'

'Oh, of course. Have you been on holiday in America recently?'

'Only briefly. I was mainly in South America.'

Dolores' eyes widened with delight. But Sophie seemed to be staring at her strangely.

'Which countries did you visit?' Dolores asked curiously.

'Not as many as I would have liked to. We stuck to the west coast basically, so we saw Colombia, Ecuador, Peru and Chile.'

'How wonderful. Did you know that I'm originally from Colombia, Sophie?'

Sophie hesitated, just for a moment. 'Oh really? I guessed you were from somewhere in Latin America, but I wasn't sure.' She laughed, but not very convincingly.

Dolores glanced briefly up the long, empty corridor again, and gently closed the doors of the linen cupboard.

'I'm heading back down to the ground floor now. I'll show you where the other storage cupboard is, if you like.'

'Thank you, that's very kind of you,' said Sophie with a smile. But her eyes told another story. They seemed to darken with reluctance as Dolores led her up towards the lift.

'So, did you learn any Spanish on your travels?' asked Dolores politely, walking as fast as her tiny legs would allow. Even Sophie appeared to struggle to keep up with her.

'Not a lot, no,' she said. Dolores noticed that she didn't elaborate. But maybe she was just out of breath.

In the lift, Dolores watched Sophie glance up at the small blinking camera.

'You know that this is possibly the only camera that's working at the moment?' She caught Sophie's eye in the mirror.

47

Neither of them mentioned the murder investigation that was rumbling on around them. But they were both thinking about it.

As the lift doors opened, it was, predictably, Michael Winterbottom's glare that they immediately encountered, visible from all the way across the foyer.

'So, if you turn right and head down this corridor, the cupboard is on your left,' whispered Dolores, before shuffling hurriedly in the direction of the vexed young manager.

'Sorry Mr Winterbottom. Sophie had gone to the wrong cupboard with the cutlery that you asked her to put away.'

Michael looked bemused. 'Cutlery? What cutlery? What on earth are you talking about, Dolores? Why would I ask Sophie to put cutlery away?'

Dolores turned back to watch the figure retreating down the corridor with a small bundle of very sharp knives in her hand, and frowned.

Chapter Sixteen

DI Sloane added the name Sarah Johnson to those already dotted around the large whiteboard in the meeting room.

'Thanks for coming in, everyone. This won't take long. I just wanted to get you all up to speed with where we are on the murder over at Lottan Lodge.'

The Inspector glanced around the room. DS Thorne had all but slipped into oblivion, surrounded as he was by notepad-wielding detectives. Though maybe his was the largest and shiniest of all notepads; Sloane would give him that.

'So, we have now established that the victim's name is Anthony Pritchard. Although he was checked into the hotel in the name of Anthony Smith. Obviously, I want some thorough background checks done on him. Was he caught up in anything insalubrious? Unless this was a case of mistaken identity, was he deliberately targeted?

Forensics have established that he was stabbed twice, once in the abdomen and once in the heart. A steak knife had been left in his chest. This has been confirmed as a knife belonging to the hotel. The time of death, according to Forensics, has to have been between six o'clock and eight o'clock on the evening on the fourteenth of February. Valentine's Day, of course. Mr Pritchard was not found until half past ten the following morning, when a hotel maid went in to clean the room. There had been significant blood loss.

We're going to need background checks on any of the staff that were on duty that evening. This will thankfully be less daunting than it sounds, as there were very few members of staff working that night. Apparently, business is quite slow at the hotel at the moment.'

Sloane pointed to the board. The name of the maid who found the victim is Dolores Gonzalez. She has worked at the hotel for years, and is probably due to retire before too long. I'm not sure why she would suddenly decide to murder a hotel guest.

Then we have Michael Winterbottom, a manager there. He's quite young, only been there a couple of years. He also saw the victim in the morning, and seemed very shocked. For someone establishing a career in hospitality, again I'm struggling to find a reason why he would commit a murder on the hotel premises.

The General Manager, George Henderson, wasn't working on the night of the murder. He claims that he was out at a restaurant with his wife and some friends. That all needs checking, of course. Obviously, none of the administrative staff, like those who work in the Accounts department, were around. But we will still need to check their alibis.

A girl named Sophie Hawkins was working on reception that evening. She's twenty-four, and has been doing a bit of travelling. She has had a couple of jobs since she's been back and had only just started working at the hotel. We need to contact her previous employers, and see what we can find out about her travels.

Sophie took over from a Fabian Dubois, a young French man, who'd worked at Lottan Lodge for nearly a year. He seems to have disappeared practically overnight a few weeks ago.

Now it appears that Anthony Pritchard had been coming to stay at the hotel for about eight months, only ever for one night at a time, every two or three weeks. I know that Mr Dubois had left Lottan Lodge by the time Mr Pritchard was murdered. But he would have come into contact with our victim on many an occasion. I'd like someone to track him down, please.

There were also a couple of members of the kitchen staff on duty that we haven't yet spoken to. According to Dolores Gonzalez, she spent most of the evening in the kitchen with them, waiting for Room Service orders, or serving the odd dinner in the more or less deserted hotel restaurant.

By the way, all of the staff are adamant that they did not visit Mr Pritchard's room on the night of the murder. The victim was staying in a room on the third floor. The only other guest on that floor on the fourteenth of February was a Bernardo Castillo. He is staying at the hotel for three weeks. He's an actor appearing in a play at the theatre in Lower Haddelton. He's got the perfect alibi really. He would have been on stage at the time of the murder, or certainly having his make-up done, I would imagine.

However, I want background checks done on him too. He's now been moved down to the second floor, so hasn't gone far.

All other guests staying at the hotel on the fourteenth of February have been contacted, and I know that the accounts of their whereabouts that evening are already being checked out. Thankfully, in terms of our investigation, there were evidently very few people on the premises that evening.

DS Thorne and I have already been to see Mr Pritchard's fiancée and have broken the news. She had reported him missing, but was very reluctant to accept that the murder victim was, in fact, her partner. However, she has now agreed to come in and identify the body for us. Her name is Arabella Winthorpe-Holmes. I'm quite curious to find out more about her and her family background.

Interestingly, we received another missing person's report for an Anthony Pritchard yesterday afternoon. This time it was from a Sarah Johnson, claiming to be his wife. Thorne and I are heading over to see her after this. If it turns out that this man did have two women on the go, we could be just about to find ourselves with a credible motive for his murder. Had one of these women found out about the other? And what exactly was Anthony Pritchard doing in a hotel room on Valentine's Day? He certainly wasn't meeting Arabella, the woman he lives with, and who'd received some beautiful Valentine's roses from him earlier that day.

Forensics did find two mobile phone chargers in the hotel room, but no phones and no ID whatsoever. There was a cheap box of chocolates and a fairly miserable bunch of flowers still there. Who were they for? And did the intended recipient ever turn up?

An envelope with £200 in it was also found in the room. It had the name Anthony handwritten in capitals on it. Why had somebody given that to him? I need someone to look very carefully into Mr Pritchard's finances. One thing is sure though, whoever killed him clearly wasn't interested in that money.

Forensics dusted everything for fingerprints, including that envelope, and they've taken exclusion prints from all the staff. Let's see what that throws up.

Unfortunately, the CCTV at the hotel is a bit hit and miss, something that could have covered up a multitude of sins. I need a couple of you to go over and retrieve whatever you can for the evening of the fourteenth. That may at least fill in a few gaps.'

Sloane carefully closed the folder on the desk in front of him and looked up, peering over his reading glasses at the detectives in front of him. 'What with the steak knife left at the scene of the crime, a possible love triangle, and faulty security cameras, we already seem to have an established means, motive and opportunity. But, as we all know, nothing is ever as it seems.'

Chapter Seventeen

The windscreen wipers seemed to make little inroad into the rain lashing against DI Sloane's car. Beside him, DS Thorne sat hunched over his phone, tapping away at the screen. Steam formed on the windows all around them.

'Well, she hasn't blocked me. That's something.'

'Why would Emily block you? And what does that even mean?'

'It just means that I wouldn't be able to see any photos she posted.'

'Is that such a bad thing? Would you want to see pictures of her going out, having fun with other people? That sounds like torture to me.'

'No, I wouldn't. But if I couldn't see, it'd be even worse. I'd be wondering what she was posting and why she was hiding it from me.'

'D'you know something? I am so glad we didn't have all this in my day. It sounds like a nightmare.'

'It's not all bad. She's just liked my beer photo.'

'Your beer photo? You posted a picture of your beer?'

'Yeah, it was a craft beer. I made it look a bit arty, of course. Nice background and all that.'

'But why?'

'It's what you do.'

'Right.'

Thorne sighed. 'I suppose I just want Emily to think I'm having a great time. You know. I want her to think I'm out and about, having a laugh. I want her to miss me.'

'I know. And I'm sure she does. Or is she just a massive fan of craft beer?' Sloane smiled.

Even Thorne had to laugh.

'It's no wonder Anthony Pritchard kept away from social media. Can you imagine? This guy could have had a whole harem of women for all we know. We could literally be at the tip of the iceberg.'

'Let's hope not. There are only so many times I want to go and break the news of his death to a poor, unsuspecting soul.' Sloane shook his head. 'And we will, of course, not be mentioning anything about other women today. Let's just deal with it as a missing person enquiry. If necessary, we'll break the news and invite her in to identify the body.'

'Not at the same time as Arabella, presumably?' Thorne laughed. 'I'd love to be a fly on the wall when they eventually have the funeral. How's that going to work?'

'It might not come to that. We might have this all wrong.' Sloane glanced at his satnav. 'Right, I think we're here now.'

They both peered out through the teeming rain at the road they had found themselves in. The grim weather did nothing to quell the grandeur of the substantial Edwardian properties all around them. All beautifully restored, their red brick facades were elegantly set off by freshly painted cladding and timbers, and large wooden window frames. Plantation shutters were everywhere. The houses stood grandly all in a row, set back from the pavement, and the neatly landscaped front gardens in front of them appeared to soak up the steady torrent with a dignified acceptance. Neat beads of rain dripped from the olive trees in large terracotta pots; pearl-like droplets danced on the elegant wrought-iron gateways.

'It's very swish around here, isn't it?' said Thorne.

'Yes. Bit of a sought-after postcode, I think.' Sloane raised his eyebrows.

'Still nowhere to park though,' said Thorne, scanning the road. 'No, actually, we're okay at this time of day. You can park here. And no pick-up trucks to negotiate round here.'

'Right,' said Sloane, as he pulled in. 'Here we go again.'

'I won't take notes,' said Thorne, popping his phone away, 'but I'm already wondering if this one bumped him off for his money. He must have had a penny or two to live somewhere like this.'

'Yes, I know. I couldn't work out what all that priceless antique furniture was doing stuffed in that small house. We might be about to find out.'

Chapter Eighteen

Bernardo Castillo stood in the foyer of Lottan Lodge and surveyed the deluge that awaited him outside. A curtain of rain drummed down onto the pavement, distorting the puddles, and cascading into the rivulets that ran down the sides of the road. It pummelled the windows of the buildings nearby, and spray danced off the roofs of passing cars. A grey blanket of low, rolling cloud raced across the sky above. Occasional gusts of wind, brisk and indiscriminate, hurled the shards of rain around erratically. His heart sank. He may have lived in this soggy country for many years now, but he had never quite adjusted to its dismal climate.

Bernardo had a matinee to do that afternoon and there was no getting out of it. He'd already used up the excuse that he usually fell back on when he was having a wobbly moment. He couldn't come down with another migraine so soon. It was only four days since he'd last had one as far as the theatre was concerned. And he didn't want to remind them about it either. So far, no one seemed to have connected his absence that evening with the murder at the hotel. In fact, he was sure that most of the cast hadn't even noticed that an understudy had played his part. He supposed that he was heavily made-up for the role. But even so.

Bernardo took a deep breath. He wasn't quite sure if his last wobbly moment had completely settled down. All his wobbly moments seemed to blend into one these days.

As he reached out reluctantly to push against the hotel's revolving door, hood up, head down, braced for the inevitable soaking that lay ahead, an arm joined his. He found himself being propelled forward in an awkwardly intimate fashion with the young hotel manager who had only yesterday so kindly offered both his discretion and a complimentary lunch.

'Are you heading in the direction of the theatre?' asked Michael, as they emerged into the damp air of the hotel forecourt. The rain pounded steadily onto the small rooftop above them, almost drowning out the sound of his voice. 'I have an umbrella and, funnily enough, I'm going that way. I don't mind sharing.'

Bernardo smiled. 'That's very kind of you, thank you. Have you finished for the day?'

'Yes,' said Michael, holding his large black umbrella above them. His height gave him a considerable advantage. 'Right, I imagine you've worked out the best route to the theatre from here by now.'

Bernardo hesitated, just for a moment. 'Oh, I already knew that. I went to school around here. I only moved away once I decided to study drama.'

'Goodness, you probably know the town better than I do. I've only been here for a couple of years. I've been renting nearby since I got this job. Nice place to go to school, I would imagine.'

'Not really.' Bernardo's eyes hardened momentarily. 'I got bullied terribly. My English wasn't great and I had a strong Spanish accent. I was just different from most of the other boys, you know. I didn't seem to fit in.' He shook his head briskly, in an attempt, perhaps, to rid himself of the unwanted images that now surfaced. 'You wouldn't believe the things that were done to me. It has probably scarred me for life if I'm honest. That's why I got into acting really. It felt like a way to be someone else, to escape being me.'

Michael nodded slowly, moving the umbrella determinedly over Bernardo, ignoring the raindrops that ran inside the collar of his jacket and down the back of his neck.

'I'm sorry to hear that, Mr Castillo,' he said. 'In my book, any bully should be given a taste of his own medicine. Don't you agree?'

'I do, Mr Winterbottom, I believe I do.'

'Call me Michael, please. I'm off-duty now. We don't have to be so formal.'

'Well Michael, thank you. And call me Bernardo. You've been very kind. I'm certainly a lot less wet than I would have been without your umbrella. I expect I shall see you tomorrow if you're working. And those detectives will be coming and going, no doubt. Any updates that I should know about? I suppose we're all suspects, aren't we?'

56

'We're all innocent until we're proven guilty, Bernardo. See you tomorrow.'

From beneath his umbrella, Michael watched the hooded figure disappear into the dark, damp alleyway that ran along the side of the theatre. He smiled, but even in the driving rain you could see the uncertainty in his eyes.

Chapter Nineteen

DS Thorpe rapped his knuckles keenly on the pretty glass insert at the centre of Sarah Johnson's gleaming front door.

'Careful,' said DI Sloane, 'That's probably been sitting there quite happily for over a century. Let's not hasten the need for any more renovation work before we've even got into the house.'

Thorne laughed. As it happened, he was just as curious as the Inspector was to see how Anthony Pritchard had divided up his furniture, and his life, between these two women.

Both men were grateful to be standing under an immaculate wooden porch. They were obliged to wait quite some time for Sarah Johnson, rain dripping from their hair, their jackets soaking up the drops of water on their shoulders after the quick dash from the car.

'I'm so sorry,' apologised Sarah, as she finally opened up her grand front door. 'I was on a conference call with the States. Couldn't escape.'

With her crisp white shirt and expensive haircut, she had a distinct air of importance. Sloane somehow sensed that she wouldn't suffer fools gladly.

'Not at all. I'm Detective Inspector Sloane and this is Detective Sergeant Thorne. I believe you've submitted a missing person's report? Are you Sarah Johnson?'

'Yes, that's me. Do come in.' She glanced down towards their feet. 'Would you mind taking your shoes off? I'll go and make us a quick cup of tea. Just leave your shoes here and come on through to the kitchen. You might want to leave your wet jackets in the hall too. But don't put them on that chair. I've just bought that. Maybe just pop them on the floor. It's very clean.'

Sloane and Thorne exchanged glances as they pulled at their laces. Sloane noted that Thorne seemed to be able to remove his shoes while still standing up. He realised that he was going to have to sit down to do it. On the floor. He didn't dare sit on the nearby new chair. Still, it gave him a great view of the teddy-bear pattern on Thorne's socks.

'Don't,' said Thorne, as he spotted Sloane's amused expression. 'Emily bought them for me. They've got sentimental value.'

'I'm just through here,' came Sarah's voice from a door at the end of the wide hallway.

Sloane gazed around as they dutifully padded through, trying not to slip on the highly polished parquet flooring. Everything in the hall was very white, from the elaborate radiator cover to the ornate bannisters. Even the staircase, with just a narrow, striped carpet running up it, was a gleaming white. Only the dainty velvet chair, with a perfectly plumped-up silk cushion, positioned with utter precision in one corner of the hall, was in a pale grey. It was immaculate, he noted as he passed it. It even smelt new. Though perhaps that was due to some sort of stain protection that had come as an extra at significant cost. Had Sarah Johnson wasted her money there, Sloane wondered? He doubted that anyone would ever get close enough to the pristine chair to mark it, never mind actually sit on it.

The large vase of red roses displayed in the centre of the lavish kitchen could not be missed. Thorne caught Sloane's eye.

'Do you take milk or sugar?' asked Sarah.

'Just milk for both of us, thanks,' said Sloane.

'If you'd like to sit yourselves over there, I'll bring it over to you.' She gestured towards the enormous corner sofa on the other side of the room. A row of pop-art prints lined the wall above it.

'Thank you for coming round so quickly about this. I hadn't expected it, to be quite honest.' Sarah placed the cups of tea onto waiting coasters. 'I did explain that Anthony isn't even due home yet. He's away with work an awful lot. It's just that I haven't been able to get through to him for a few days, which is very unusual. I'm slightly worried that I'm wasting police time, with you two detectives sitting here. Though I do have another work call that I need to be on in twenty minutes or so, so I won't be taking up too much of your time.'

Sloane scoured a selection of framed photographs on the wall beside him.

'Is that your husband there?' he asked, nodding towards a picture of a sun-drenched beach wedding. The now familiar figure of Anthony Pritchard, relaxed in white linen, smiled broadly at him. Sarah, graceful and willowy in a simple satin dress, beamed as she held her neat bouquet aloft. They were both barefoot on fine white sand, with the sunset reflected in the sea behind them. It was all picture postcard perfect. Or too good to be true?

'Yes, that's him. Well, that's from six years ago. We got married out in the Caribbean. I'd wanted a big family wedding, the whole works, but Anthony doesn't have much of a family and he was worried that it would all be a bit one-sided. He was right in the end. It was bliss. I'd do it all again.' She smiled dreamily.

Sloane was aware of Thorne leaning down to look at his socks. Which probably wasn't helping.

He cleared his throat. 'Mrs Pritchard, I'm very sorry to have to tell you this, but a body has been discovered at a hotel in Lower Haddelton. We believe that it may be your husband, though he was checked in under the name of Anthony Smith.'

'A hotel? In Lower Haddelton? He grew up in the town, but why in the world would he check into a hotel there? Which hotel was it?'

'Lottan Lodge,' said Sloane.

'Lottan Lodge? Anthony wouldn't be seen dead in a place like that.'

A silence descended upon the room. Sloane avoided eye contact with Thorne.

But then Sarah laughed sardonically. 'I rest my case, officers. Let's just say that my husband liked the finer things in life. I think you've just told me all I need to know. Look, I'm starting to wish I'd never contacted you. This is all getting a bit over-dramatic. Why don't we give this a few more days, and hopefully Anthony will turn up? His phone's probably broken or something.'

'I'm afraid that it is looking like this could be your husband, Mrs Pritchard. I know that this might be a bit of a shock. Is there anyone that can be with you?'

'Firstly, it's Ms Johnson. I've never liked to think of myself as my husband's chattel. Secondly, I really do think that this is all a ridiculous misunderstanding. But yes, our au pair will be back in a bit. She picks up my son from school, and then he has a swimming lesson. Apart from that, I will be addressing the

Board of the company that I work for in approximately ten minutes. So, if you gentlemen don't mind.'

'Of course. Here's my card. But we will be in touch again shortly.'

'Thank you, officers. I'm sure we'll get to the bottom of all this very quickly.'

Despite her impending meeting, Sarah Johnson stood for quite some time at her front door and stared after the two detectives, even as they gratefully pulled their car doors closed against the rain that still fell.

Chapter Twenty

February 19

In the station office, DI Sloane sat transfixed in front of his computer screen, oblivious to the occasional ringing of a phone, or the tapping of keyboards and quiet chats going on around him.

'Well, well, well,' he said, 'That's interesting.'

DS Thorne looked up from his phone. 'What is?' he said absently.

'Are you alright? You look a bit out of sorts,' asked Sloane.

'Yeah, I'm fine. Sorry, I was just checking Emily's location and it's knocked me for six.'

'You were checking Emily's location? How? Do you have that tracking option set up?'

'No, there's an app where everyone can see where all their friends are. Well, at least where they were the last time they posted a photo on that app.'

'My God, there is literally no privacy these days. If this Anthony Pritchard was living a double life, he must have had to work very hard at it.'

'I know. And I know it sounds like I'm stalking Emily now, but it's just so difficult not to look.'

'Yeah, I can understand that. So where is she anyway?'

'It looks like she's at a hotel down in Brighton. What is she doing there?'

'She's probably with friends or something.'

Sloane could see the anguish written all over his sergeant's face. 'Look, d'you want to go for a beer later? We'll talk about it then.'

Thorne nodded miserably.

Sloane pointed to his computer screen. 'Right, look at all this. Arabella Winthorpe-Holmes has got a very interesting family background. Her grandfather was a Baron, and his father before that. They had a stately pile out in Berkshire. Seems they managed to keep it going until the 1950s. Longer than a lot of these places survived by all accounts. There's loads on here about it. Interestingly, it was used as a military hospital in both world wars. Anyway, her grandmother was some wealthy American, clearly brought in to save the day. Which kept things going for a while. But the house got sold off and flattened by developers in the end. When her great-grandparents died, the tax bills were just too high for the family to keep the place on. Apparently, there's nothing remotely aristocratic about the 1960s office blocks that sit on the land these days.'

'But there must still be a bit of money in the family. It can't all have just disappeared.'

'You're right. They had to de-camp to their London residence after that. But it was in Belgravia. So worth an absolute fortune. And there was clearly enough money to maintain that as a family home. Well, until two years ago anyway.'

'What happened two years ago?'

'Well, up to that point, with Arabella's grandparents now gone, her father, The Honourable George Winthorpe-Holmes, and her mother, Alice, owned the property in Belgravia outright, and were residing there full-time.'

'Well, Arabella seems to have come down in the world. Where did it all go horribly wrong? Has there been a family rift or something?'

'Well, this is the thing. Two years ago, her parents were out on a safari in Africa somewhere. And both died.'

'You're joking. What a way to go. What was it? Leopards or something?'

'No, Thorne. They weren't mauled by wildcats, or trampled by elephants for that matter. They were involved in some sort of collision. Their jeep overturned. Which is no less sad, of course.'

'Yeah, that's terrible. But I still don't understand why Arabella isn't living in luxury.'

'Yes, I haven't got to the bottom of that yet. Even if her parents hadn't left a will, probate would surely have gone through by now. There certainly doesn't seem to be an older brother, or even a younger brother, who could have inherited it all. There is an older sister. She's married and lives up in

Scotland. It sounds like she's part of the whole tweed-wearing, deer-stalking brigade.'

'It would be a bit mean to leave all your money to one daughter and not the other.'

'Well, we are seeing Arabella later, once she's formally identified the body. I do feel sorry for her, but we are going to have to ask a few more questions about her life with Anthony Pritchard if we're going to make any headway with cracking this case. The leads aren't exactly coming in thick and fast at the moment.'

Thorne glanced at his computer. 'Funny you should say that. Forensics have just sent something through.'

He leant closely towards the screen as he read. 'Right. The murder weapon had no fingerprints on it at all. But the envelope stuffed with all that cash had a number of prints on it. And they were a clear match with someone at the hotel. Michael Winterbottom. The envelope was covered in that young manager's fingerprints.'

'Sir,' came a voice from across the room.

'McArdle, what have you got for me?' asked Sloane.

'We've just been sent across some of the CCTV footage that they're trying to retrieve at Lottan Lodge. They've got some from the lift that evening. So far, the only person to go up to the third floor is Michael Winterbottom. He uses the lift at ten past seven and is carrying a tray. He doesn't get back into the lift to come down until fifteen minutes later.'

'Gotcha,' said Thorne.

'Maybe,' said Sloane. 'But we need to see the footage of him coming back down. You don't stab someone twice like that and not get at least a bit of blood on you, surely? One thing is for sure though. We need Michael Winterbottom in for questioning right now.'

Chapter Twenty-One

Dolores slowly descended the narrow concrete steps that led down to the hotel's dim underground car park. She didn't tend to drive to work usually. She quite enjoyed getting the bus really. More often than not, she'd fall into conversation with a fellow passenger, even if she tried really hard not to. It certainly passed the time. Dolores lived a little way out from Lower Haddelton, but it suited her. She certainly wouldn't want to be bumping into colleagues or hotel guests when she was off-duty and out and about.

But she had brought her car in today as she'd had a very early shift this morning. And Mr Henderson was very good about letting the staff park at the hotel. There were always plenty of spaces these days.

The windowless car park, with its grimy, concrete walls and low ceiling, was always very dingy. The air was unfailingly cold and dank. The dim, sporadic lighting cast indistinct shadows, vague and misshapen, in all directions; to Dolores, they looked like eerie contorted figures, poised to pounce. Her footsteps echoed loudly in the silence. The sound of them seemed to bounce indiscriminately off the bleak walls all around her, almost as though she weren't alone. She shivered and felt for the keys in her bag.

'Dolores,' came a voice from some distance behind her. She didn't need to turn round.

'Sophie?'

She could hear the girl's ragged breathing, and tentative footsteps approaching, reverberating all around her.

'Sophie, listen. Whatever you are planning to do, you don't have to do it. It could ruin your life. It could ruin other people's lives. Think carefully.'

The footsteps came to a halt just behind Dolores. The irregular, laboured breaths seemed to surround her; she could feel them, like you felt the first gusts of an approaching storm. And you knew in that moment that there was no turning back.

As Dolores waited uneasily, rooted to the spot, her shoulders rigid, her unseeing eyes wide with fear, she sensed a stillness. The calm before the storm maybe? A silence seemed to unfurl all around her as she stood there, resigned to her fate. She gripped the keys in her hand instinctively yet dispiritedly. In a nearby corner, single drops of water fell from the damp, concrete ceiling, one after the other, hitting a puddle with force; an unhurried, steady dripping, a rhythmic marking of the time that passed.

Dolores had heard that your life was supposed to flash before your eyes just before you died. But, for her, it wasn't going to be an automatic process, forced upon her haphazardly, without her having any say on the matter. She wasn't going to be a passive recipient of random memories; a casual passenger on a whirlwind tour of times gone by. The final pictures in her head would be specific; she was going to be fully in charge of the moments she would relive; they would consist solely of the precious times spent with her husband and her daughter. Dolores allowed herself to wonder if they'd had a tip-off and were waiting for her right now.

She smiled down at the emerald ring on her finger and thought of her wedding day. In the simple white dress that her mother had cobbled together, pieces of satin and lace lovingly crafted into a demure high-neck frock, she had never felt so glamorous. Or so in love. Just looking at Juan had made her go weak at the knees. And when she'd reached him at the altar, the look on his face had told her that he undoubtedly felt the same. There was so much to celebrate. They'd wanted to announce their love from the rooftops. Back then, they hadn't really had a penny to their names, but they'd been determined to have the whole village there that evening, dancing, eating and drinking under the stars that sparkled gloriously in the night sky above them. Though Juan had always said afterwards that he hadn't noticed any stars, not with Dolores around. She had outshone them all.

Dolores remembered the day that Elena had been born, seeing her tiny face for the first time, red and damp, disoriented, adjusting to her new surroundings. She'd seemed so delicate, so fragile. Juan had laughed and kissed Dolores when she'd said she wished she had a pouch to keep Elena in, like a kangaroo. She'd wanted to keep her safe for ever. But she hadn't, of course.

Strangely, so focused was Dolores on the images that she had conjured up so determinedly, she didn't immediately notice that the quiet had been broken by the sound of distant muffled sobs and hurried footsteps, growing ever fainter. And when Dolores dared to turn around, the shadowy figures that met her were silent and unmoving.

Chapter Twenty-Two

Arabella dabbed at her eyes with the tissue that DI Sloane had passed her.

'Thank you for coming in to talk to us again, Arabella. I know that this must be an extremely distressing time for you. We appreciate you carrying out the formal identification of the body of your fiancé. I want you to know that this will really help us move forward now with this case.'

Arabella nodded, the crumpled tissue held to her nose.

'Can you think of anyone who would have wanted to murder Anthony?'

She shook her head, tears falling anew.

'Did he have any issues with his job, his colleagues? Any money problems that you know of?'

Arabella sighed. 'That's just it. We had been struggling a little. We're just renting at the moment, but even paying the rent was a bit of a stretch. But things were about to change. It was just that he didn't know yet. I'm so worried now that he'd gone to a loan shark or something, and had got himself into trouble. I should have told him.' She began to weep.

'You should have told him what?'

'I'm going to come into a lot of money later this year, once I turn twenty-six. But I had never told Anthony. I wanted to be sure that he loved me for who I am, not for my money.'

'That's understandable. Is this an inheritance that's coming to you?'

'Yes. My parents died a couple of years ago, and it's just my sister and me now. They did leave a will, and are splitting everything between the two of us. But, well, the thing is, I was a bit of a wild child. I was expelled from two boarding schools, and got up to all sorts of mischief really. Anyway, my poor exasperated mother really read up on the psychology and neuroscience behind all my dreadful impulsive adolescent behaviour. She would always tell me that my neurons were busy being pruned, as we all had far too many of them for a while, and that my brain would settle down around the age of twenty-six. I think she took great comfort from that. It's so sad that she didn't live to see my new improved pre-frontal cortex.' Arabella smiled wanly.

'So, your inheritance comes through when you turn twenty-six?'

'Exactly. I nearly told Anthony so many times. Especially when we started thinking about our wedding. Anthony loved the idea of a beach wedding out in the Caribbean. He had no idea that we were actually going to be able to afford something like that. He thought that my family had pretty much cut me off, and that my inheritance amounted to the bits of furniture I'd managed to salvage.'

'I suppose it's difficult for you to work at the moment, with the little one?' said Sloane.

'Yes.' She hesitated briefly. 'I went to drama school, and did a bit of acting, mainly theatre work. It's not really something I can do without paying an enormous amount of money for childcare. And Anthony was away a lot obviously.'

'Do you have any idea why he would have been in that hotel that evening?'

Arabella shook her head miserably. 'I just can't understand it. It must have been something to do with work. Maybe he had to meet a business associate there?'

'According to our checks, Anthony worked for an insurance company in Croydon. Is that correct?'

'Yes, that's right. The headquarters are there. But he has meetings all over the country too.'

Sloane wasn't sure how he managed to keep his expression neutral. He didn't dare look at Thorne.

'I'm so sorry, but I do just have to ask you where you were on the night of the fourteenth of February.'

'Of course. I totally understand. I did, in fact, go out that evening. Just to the gym for around a couple of hours. Jackie, over the road, had Henry for the night. She has a travel cot that we both use. I look after her little boy sometimes, when she wants to escape for an evening out. I can give you the name of my gym if you need it.'

'Thank you, that would be useful.'

Arabella wiped at her eyes and sighed. 'Well, I'm going to have all this money now, and no one to spend it on. And I don't suppose either of you are in need of an engagement ring, are you?'

As much as his heart went out to Thorne in the face of this untimely, throwaway remark, Sloane found it rather strange that this bereaved young woman would be offering up something of such sentimental value so readily. Thorne's teddy-bear socks came to mind. Surely, you would want to be holding on to anything you had that reminded you of the person you had lost? Yes, he thought, it was very strange behaviour indeed.

Sloane didn't like to think of himself as a cynic. He was always prepared to give people the benefit of the doubt until the evidence proved otherwise. But had Thorne been right? Could it be that the person who had come forward to claim the late Anthony Pritchard as their own, had in fact murdered him? This woman, in whom he had witnessed a whole raft of emotions, had been to drama school. She'd performed on stage. Could it be that her bewilderment and distress were all just an act? He thought of Bernardo Castillo. How strange, he thought, that two of the possible suspects in this case were actors. He even wondered if their paths had ever crossed.

The problem was, of course, that Sarah Johnson had now staked her claim too. Well, not that she had agreed to for now. But she had. She just didn't know it as yet. And she had just as much of a reason to kill Anthony Pritchard as Arabella did.

Mind you, thought Sloane, Michael Winterbottom's fingerprints on that envelope might blow all these theories about scorned women right out of the water. Who knew? One thing was certain though. This case was not turning out to be straightforward. *Quelle surprise.*

Chapter Twenty-Three

February 20

In the interview room at Haddelton police station, Michael Winterbottom looked like a rabbit caught in headlights. He sat rigidly across the table from DI Sloane and DS Thorne, his gaze alternating between the tape recorder to his side and the two detectives in front of him. Sloane observed the beads of sweat forming on his pale forehead; he noticed him swallow conspicuously; he certainly didn't seem to know what to do with his hands.

'Mr Winterbottom, thank you for coming in today to speak to us again. We have a few more questions that we would like to put to you, further to updates in our enquiry.'

Michael nodded his head. 'Of course,' he managed to say.

'We wondered if you would be able to clear up two matters for us. In the first instance, your fingerprints have been found on an envelope full of money in Mr Pritchard's room. Can you explain how this could have come about?'

'Mr Pritchard? Who's he?' Michael looked confused.

'That's the name of the man who was killed in Room 304. So, can you confirm that you were unaware of his real name?'

'I had no idea. He always signed in as Mr Smith and paid his bills in cash.'

'Mr Winterbottom, was it you who was providing all this ready cash? And why were you doing that?'

Michael shook his head. 'I always put out a pile of envelopes on the desk in reception. It seems to go down quite well with customers, even in this day and age. That would probably explain it.'

Sloane noticed him breathe a small sigh of relief.

'The thing is, Mr Winterbottom, you have shown up on the hotel CCTV, using the lift up to the third floor on the evening of the fourteenth of February. You were carrying a tray.'

'Are you sure? George Henderson had told me that the hotel cameras needed a complete overhaul. The camera in the lift has been very on and off. I thought it had given up the ghost a couple of weeks ago.'

Sloane laid a photograph on the table in front of Michael and leant towards the tape recorder. 'I am showing Mr Winterbottom an image of himself in the hotel lift at ten past seven on the fourteenth of February.'

Michael dropped his gaze and stared at the photograph.

'Mr Winterbottom. There were only two guests staying on the third floor that evening; Mr Anthony Smith, as you knew him, and Mr Castillo. We understand that Mr Castillo was on stage at the time. No order has been put through the system. Who were you taking the tray up to?'

Michael sat in silence for a few moments.

'It was Mr Smith.' His bottom lip began to quiver and a solitary tear ran down his ashen face.

'Was there a steak knife on that tray? It's not completely visible in our images.'

'No, definitely not. There was a spoon for the gazpacho soup and a bread knife for the roll. But nothing sharper than that. Nothing that I could have murdered Mr Smith with.'

'What's troubling us, Mr Winterbottom, is that your fingerprints were also found on some of the £20 notes in the envelope. So, unless you are going to tell me that you personally place a pile of cash on the reception desk for guests to help themselves to, you've got some significant explaining to do.'

Chapter Twenty-Four

Sophie checked her phone for the fiftieth time that day. She couldn't believe that Fabian was ignoring her like this. Or maybe she could. She never seemed to have any luck with men. Perhaps she just fell for the wrong sort. The exotic, unconventional types. It certainly hadn't taken long to fall under Fabian's spell when she'd found herself teaching him English a few months back, her first job since she'd got back from her travels.

Sophie had to admit that she'd found Fabian completely mesmerising from the word go. He'd really looked like something out of a magazine when he'd walked into the classroom that first day with the other students. With his soft caramel-coloured eyes, his dark stubble, and his silky, dishevelled hair, he was very easy on the eye. Coming from Paris, he'd seemed very chic and sophisticated to Sophie at first. Yet, as she'd soon discovered, he had a wonderfully self-deprecating sense of humour. She'd soon found him totally irresistible. Of course, his accent was adorable. She'd often watched his lips as he spoke, wondering what it would be like to kiss them. Mind you, Fabian was charming with all of them really. In fact, he seemed to have turned flirting into an art form. You really felt that you were the most fascinating person in the world when his attention was on you.

Sophie had started joining her students for drinks after classes. She was no older than most of them, and she missed the excitement of travelling, of meeting people from all over the world. And it had meant that she got to spend more time in the company of Fabian. They'd laughed so much on their evenings out. He had an infectious *joie de vivre* that she'd found utterly captivating; they all had. He'd often entertained them with anecdotes about the guests and the staff at the hotel he was employed at. In the end, she'd felt that she knew them all personally.

It was Fabian who had put her up to all this, of course. And now, when she needed him, he had vanished without trace.

Chapter Twenty-Five

Michael Winterbottom gazed forlornly at the image of himself in the hotel lift, lying on the desk in front of him.

'Mr Winterbottom,' said Sloane.

'Please, call me Michael.'

'Michael, you need to be thinking about getting yourself legal representation. This is a murder we are investigating.'

'I realise that,' Michael said dejectedly. 'But the thing is, I didn't do it. I wanted to do it, I'll admit that. I certainly had a good enough reason to kill him. But I didn't. You see I'm a weak man, Inspector. I was too busy worrying about my job at the hotel. I wasn't strong enough to stand up to Anthony Smith. Or whatever his name was. And I am glad that he's dead. It certainly removes a whole load of problems from my life. But I didn't kill him.'

Michael sighed. 'You know, I'd sometimes thought about how I could kill him. Make it look like an accident. Put some rat poison in his full English breakfast; push him out of the window; hold him down in the bath. But stab him? Never.' Michael laughed wryly, wiping at the tears that now streamed down his washed-out face. 'Fortunately, in this line of work, unlike your good selves, I don't have to deal with blood very often. You see, I'm extremely squeamish. I can't stand the sight of blood. Detectives, if I had stabbed Anthony Smith, I would have been found passed out on the floor next to him. In fact, that's exactly what happened the following morning when Dolores pulled me into his room and I saw his blood-spattered body.'

'Well, we'll have to take your word for it about all this squeamishness for now. But, can I ask, do you fantasise about murdering all your hotel guests, or was it just this one in particular?' Sloane arched an eyebrow.

Michael looked horrified. 'What must you think of me? Detectives, you need to know that Anthony Smith was an exceptionally cruel man. He had put me in an impossible situation.' He began to sob loudly.

Sloane passed him a tissue. 'In your own time, Michael. We're all ears.' He could sense the impatience in Thorne, sitting next to him, pen poised for action.

Michael took a deep breath. 'He was blackmailing me. Every time he came to the hotel, he expected another payment. And he kept wanting more. Far more than I could afford.'

'Why was he blackmailing you, Michael?'

'It was all a terrible misunderstanding, really. I'd been getting such mixed messages. I guess I just got the wrong end of the stick. But I really did think that he liked me. It was simply a genuine mistake.' Michael dabbed at his eyes.

'Am I right in understanding that you thought Anthony might be interested in you?'

'Anthony Smith? Goodness. No. Absolutely not. And I certainly wasn't interested in him either, I can tell you that.'

'Right. So, what did happen?'

'There was a lovely young French man who worked here until quite recently. Fabian. We really hit it off. He had one of those magnetic personalities, you know? I think I sort of fell under his spell really. I was so drawn to him. And I truly believed that my feelings were reciprocated. Anyway, one quiet evening, I bumped into Fabian on one of the upper floor corridors. We chatted and laughed for a bit, and I suddenly decided that it was time to make my move. Well, one of us had to, didn't we? Or so I thought at the time.

Sadly, it didn't go quite as I had expected. Fabian nearly threw a left hook at me. I was mortified, of course. I tried to apologise, to explain my actions, but he couldn't seem to get away quickly enough. Though he was kind enough to say not to worry, and that he wasn't going to say anything to anyone. I felt so embarrassed, as you can imagine. I was dreading seeing him after what had happened. But he didn't seem to hold it against me. I think he understood that ours was perhaps an ambivalent situation. In fact, he was always perfectly pleasant to me, right up to when he left. It was as though it had never happened really.'

'So, what did all this have to do with Anthony?'

Michael's face darkened. 'Unfortunately, of all the people in the world, it had to be Anthony who emerged from the lift at the end of the corridor and witnessed the incident. He stood and watched as I leant in to kiss Fabian. He saw how Fabian retaliated and made his escape. I could tell from the sly, smug look on Anthony's face, as he got closer and closer, that this wasn't going to end well.'

'So, what happened then?'

'When he got to me, he sneered and said that I was done for. He made that gesture, you know, cutting his throat with his hand. I was terrified. I was literally shaking in my boots. My job is everything to me. I don't really have anything else in my life.' Michael's eyes filled up again and he dabbed despondently at them.

'Take your time, Michael.' Sloane moved the box of tissues towards him.

'Anthony seemed to relish the idea that he held my fate in his hands. It was torture. I can't tell you how relieved I was when he eventually said that I could buy his silence. I'd have done anything at that point. At the time, I'd thought it was a one-off payment. I had a little bit tucked away in my savings account. I don't really spend that much money. I've got no one to spend it on.' He pulled a tissue from the box.

'Anyway, he started coming to the hotel every two or three weeks. And every time he came, he demanded more money from me. It all seemed to be getting out of control really. I just wanted the whole situation to go away.'

As Sloane and Thorne stared uncertainly at Michael, weeping quietly in front of them, there was a sharp knock on the door.

'Sir, something you might want to see.'

Sloane nodded and reached for the note being offered to him.

'Well, well, well,' he said, as his eyes skimmed over the words he held in his lap.

'According to French police, Fabian Dubois was reported missing by his family a couple of days ago. He hasn't been seen alive for over three weeks.'

He looked up at Michael, who was now as white as a sheet. 'So, the man you allegedly accosted is missing, and the hotel guest that witnessed the incident is dead. Mr Winterbottom, I suggest that you get yourself a very good lawyer.'

Chapter Twenty-Six

February 21

'Can I have some quiet for a moment, please?'

The hum of chatter in the meeting room halted abruptly, and the assembled detectives turned towards DI Sloane, who wrote the word 'Missing' beneath the photograph of Fabian Dubois on the large whiteboard next to him.

'Thanks. And thank you for all coming in here for a quick update. I won't keep you too long.'

He turned to DS Thorne. 'By the way, any news on Sarah Johnson yet?'

'Yes, she's agreed to identify the body this morning. She seems to be coming round to the idea that Anthony Smith may be her missing husband. She hasn't had any contact at all with him for a week now. She was definitely starting to sound a bit worried on the phone earlier. I've asked her to come in and speak to us a bit later, if that works, Sir?'

'Absolutely. I'd love to put a few more questions to her. She is clearly a very intelligent, successful woman. I find it hard to believe that she had no idea that her husband had this whole other life going on.'

'What I can't understand is that the two women in Anthony Pritchard's life are like chalk and cheese,' said Thorne. 'Sarah is quite intimidating, a force to be reckoned with, while Arabella seems so much more easy-going. A bit scatty almost. And then there's the age difference. Sarah is almost ten years older than Arabella.'

'Well, there's one glaringly obvious thing that Sarah and Arabella do have in common. Money. And a lot of it. Was Anthony about to divorce Sarah, fleece her for half of all that she'd worked hard to achieve, and then move on to enjoy the spoils of Arabella's not insignificant trust fund? What if Sarah had got wind of this? If there was no pre-nuptial signed, was Sarah desperate enough to make sure Anthony didn't see these plans through?'

'Maybe,' said Thorne. 'But I still think the butler did it.' he laughed.

Sloane smiled. 'McArdle, how's it going with the CCTV footage at the hotel?'

'Right, well it turns out there is a working security camera over a door at the back of the hotel leading into the kitchen - a very vulnerable spot obviously. It covers part of the kitchen and we've picked up the kitchen staff working away at the ovens between six and eight o'clock. There were only two of them on duty that night. But there is no sign of anyone entering or leaving via that door on the evening in question.

We've also got plenty of footage from the lift now. Michael Winterbottom is not the only person to have gone up to the third floor in our time frame. At just after twenty-five to seven, a young female travels up to that floor. She comes back down around fifteen minutes later. It's going to be pretty difficult to identify her. She's wearing a sweatshirt with the hood up. She keeps her head down and faces away from the camera. Her sweatshirt is pretty distinctive, though. Turquoise and white. I've got an image here for you. She's not a hotel guest. We've pretty much accounted for the whereabouts of the few people who were booked in for that night. Most of them are seen using the lift to get down to the foyer and go on out to restaurants, not returning until much later.

Dolores Gonzales is seen in the lift going up to the first floor a couple of times, bringing trays up to guests. Of these two guests, one was on a lengthy conference call that went on beyond eight o'clock. His participation has been verified by a number of other people on that call. The other guest was only there because she had sprained her ankle that afternoon and couldn't drive home. She seemed quite happy just to have been able to put her feet up and rest. A doctor has confirmed the sprain.

So, I think we can rule them both out in terms of the murder of Anthony Pritchard. They were both very grateful for the room service provided by Dolores Gonzalez.'

'Did anyone get anything interesting on Dolores?'

Thorne nodded. 'I did a bit of looking into her. As we know, she's originally from Colombia. Came over here around twenty-five years ago with her husband and a daughter. Both now dead. Her daughter died twenty years ago. They lived in Lower Haddelton when they first came to England. The daughter was the same age as Anthony Pritchard, who was also living in Lower Haddelton at the time.'

'That's interesting. How did she die?'

'Well, she actually died over in Colombia. She was there on a holiday, I think. It says that she died of misadventure on the death certificate. Dolores' husband died nearly three years later. That was a heart attack.'

'Has Anthony Pritchard ever been to Colombia? Was he there when the daughter died?'

'No. There's no record of him ever having travelled there. Or anywhere nearby.'

'Okay. Maybe there's a possible connection there. Not sure if we're clutching at straws though. She certainly didn't mention her to us. But then, why would she? Also, given Dolores' age, and rather frail condition, I can't really see her dashing around the hotel, overpowering guests and stabbing them frenziedly to death. I suppose you never know though.'

Sloane turned back to look at the whiteboard. 'What about Sophie Hawkins? Have we got anything more on her? Could she be the young female seen in the lift heading up to the third floor? Bryant, weren't you looking into her background?'

'Yep, and there was something interesting. It turns out that, before she started at Lottan Lodge, she was teaching English to Fabian Dubois. Now missing, of course. He was doing an evening course once a week at the college in Lower Haddelton. I don't think she ever thought to mention that to us. The funny thing is that she lives up towards North London. But since she's been back from travelling, both her jobs been in Lower Haddelton. It's a bit of a trek to say the least.'

'I really don't think there's anything remotely sinister about Sophie Hawkins. But I'm very happy to conduct another interview,' said Thorne, grinning.

Sloane smiled. 'I do think that we need to ask a few more questions there. But I'll come too. In the interests of balance. Good cop, bad cop and all that.'

Thorne glanced at the board. 'So, are we thinking that Michael Winterbottom probably did it?'

McArdle looked up from his notes. 'The only thing I would say is that we have a clear image of Michael heading down in the lift at twenty-five past seven. His uniform is identical to when he travelled up fifteen minutes earlier. His jacket remains unbuttoned and his white shirt is clearly visible. There are no blood spatters to be seen on it. It's pristine, in fact.'

'Also,' said Sloane, 'what happened to the tray he supposedly brought up to Anthony? There was no tray found in the room the following morning. What with the unidentified female in the lift, I'm starting to feel that there was a lot more going on up on that third floor than we realise.'

He closed the file on the desk in front of him. 'Right, keep at it everyone. Thorne, let's see what Sarah Johnson has got to say.'

But Thorne wasn't listening. He had his head bowed over his phone.'

'Thorne?'

'Well,' said Thorne, looking up rather excitedly. 'You're not going to believe this. That was a text from downstairs. They've just had a call from Bernardo Castillo. The Spanish bloke who was also staying on the third floor the night of the murder. He wants to come in and make a new statement. He says he's heard that Michael Winterbottom has become the prime suspect. Apparently, he wants to set the record straight.'

Chapter Twenty-Seven

DI Sloane watched Sarah Johnson as she described her job to DS Thorne. With her subtly highlighted blonde hair, beautifully tailored clothes, and the cloud of expensive perfume that surrounded her, she looked at ease with the wealth she clearly enjoyed. She seemed remarkably composed for someone who had just identified the body of her dead husband. Perhaps she was in shock, he wondered. She certainly appeared to have been in denial up to this point. Or maybe she just found it easier to deal with the whole sorry affair with her professional mask on, efficient, business-like, unwilling to show a chink in her armour. He wondered if she'd go home after this and howl into a cushion.

Sloane had been unable to detect any hint of a souring in the marriage between this calm and collected woman and the man who had been stabbed to death last week. She seemed to have adored him; didn't have a bad word to say about him. From the whirlwind romance nearly seven years ago, the dream wedding and honeymoon that followed, to their delight at the birth of their son, Oliver, five years ago, and their pride in the house that they'd so lovingly renovated, there just didn't seem to be any red flags, anything at all to suggest that Sarah Johnson would suddenly decide to brutally murder her husband.

Unless she was an exceedingly good liar, of course. Unless she did, in fact, know about Anthony's life with another woman. Unless she had worked out that he didn't, in fact, travel the country on important business, but remained, day in, day out, at his desk in an office in Croydon, looking at insurance claims. And unless she had discovered that he had been regularly checking into a hotel in Lower Haddelton for the last few months.

The Inspector glanced at his notes. 'Sarah, can I ask you, where were you on the night of the murder?'

Sarah turned to him with an indignant stare. 'I hope you're not implying what I think you are.'

'We have to ask everybody. We need to be able to rule you out.'

'Of course, sorry.' She smiled briefly. 'I met up with a few other ladies for a drink. We all knew that we were going to find ourselves alone that evening. You know, for the usual reasons; divorced, beheaded, died, away on business, that sort of thing. There's a great new cocktail place in Lower Haddelton, near the market square. You have to book, and the cocktails cost a fortune. But it's a great place and we all thought we deserved a nice night out.'

'So you were, coincidentally, in Lower Haddelton, on the night your husband was murdered?'

'Yes. Ironic, isn't it? Anyway, I'm sure that my friends and the staff there will be able to confirm everything. Our table was booked for eight o'clock. They might even have me on a CCTV camera somewhere.'

'Thank you, that's very helpful. We'll let you get home now. Unless you have any questions for us?'

Sloane noted that Sarah was already buttoning up her coat.

'No. I think I just need to go home now and digest all of this. I really have no idea what Anthony was doing in that hotel. It must have been something to do with his job.'

The Inspector hesitated. 'Ms Johnson, can I show you an image we have of someone in the hotel lift that evening? Possibly heading up towards Anthony's room.'

Sloane placed the photograph of the young, hooded female in front of Sarah. He observed her as she leant forward. He watched as she stared silently. He saw how she narrowed her eyes, and how deep ridges formed in her forehead; how her face blanched.

'I don't believe this. I feel sick,' she said slowly.

Sarah raised her stricken face to meet Sloane's eye. 'I'd know that hoodie anywhere. That's Luciana. Our au pair.'

Chapter Twenty-Eight

February 22

Bernardo Castillo could feel himself shaking as he stood at the window of his hotel room, just back from his trip to the police station. He'd wondered why he hadn't seen Michael around the hotel. It had been the older lady, Dolores, who'd brought him up his gazpacho soup on a tray before he'd set off for the theatre two evenings ago. In fact, it was Dolores who had filled him in on what had been going on. He was quite grateful that she hadn't seemed to be worried about any sort of staff confidentiality issues. She'd chatted away for quite some time actually. He'd suspected that she was delighted at the chance to be speaking her own language. Fortunately, his soup had been cold to start with.

Bernardo had been horrified to learn of what Michael was going through; the police interviews, the search for a lawyer, the need to take a few days off from work. And it was all because of him. It was all his fault. He'd realised that evening that it was time to come clean.

He couldn't let an innocent man go to the gallows. And Michael Winterbottom was innocent. He was sure of that. He felt it in his bones. Michael had been the only person to show him any warmth and kindness in his hour of need. Men like that didn't go around stabbing people to death. Even someone like Anthony Pritchard. And God knows, if anyone deserved to have a blade plunged into them, it was Anthony Pritchard.

Bernardo hadn't recognised him immediately when he'd got into the lift with him that afternoon. It had been an awfully long time, after all. He'd smiled politely as they'd stood there, heading slowly upwards towards the third floor, rather pleased to find himself in the company of such a startlingly attractive man. Bernardo had spotted the flowers and chocolates in the man's hands. Naturally, with looks like those, this Adonis wasn't going to be alone on a Valentine's Day evening.

Unlike himself.

Bernardo had not been able to face going on stage that night. He'd already made his excuses with the theatre. Like the handsome man in the lift, he too had held a plastic supermarket bag in his hand. But his had contained a bottle of fine Spanish red wine. And Bernardo was fully intending to drink all of it, on his own, in his room. And have a good cry too probably. Well, that's what you did when your heart was broken, didn't you?

It was only after they'd arrived at the third floor and Bernardo was forlornly making his way along the corridor that the handsome man had spoken to him.

'I think this belongs to you,' he'd said from behind him. When Bernardo turned around, Anthony had picked up his scarf from the floor and was holding it out for him.

'Oh, thank you,' Bernardo had said, 'how kind of you.'

And then he'd seen the dawning recognition in the man's eye, the sneer that had slowly contorted his face. And it had all come back to him. The mimicking of his accent, the school books down toilets, his head down toilets, the abject fear that he had felt just going into school that year.

'Well, hello,' Anthony had said in an exaggerated Spanish accent, prolonging the h with all his might. 'I remember you. Pedro, wasn't it? Still haven't gone back to your own country then?'

Bernardo had spent years practising his retorts, planning exactly what he would say if he ever saw Anthony Pritchard again. He'd worked out his lines perfectly, and knew how he would coolly gain the upper hand before dismissing the shamefaced man's pathetic, grovelling apologies.

'Hope they managed to potty train you in the end. We wouldn't want any more little accidents, would we?' Anthony smirked.

Bernardo had felt his face burn with humiliation. He'd almost felt the trickle down his leg, and seen the small pool at his feet. He'd been that terrified fifteen-year-old again, cornered in the boys' toilets with jeering faces all around him, Anthony Pritchard holding the lit cigarette like a pen, waving it around above Bernardo's bare arm.

Standing in that hotel corridor, it had taken every ounce of Bernardo's strength not to take out the wine bottle and smash it over Anthony's head. But that wasn't him. And he had known there and then that he wasn't going to emerge victorious from some war of words. There wasn't going to be any admission of guilt or wrong-doing from Anthony. There was no remorse there. There would be no attempt at justification, no seeking of atonement. Not from this man. A man without a heart. A man who clearly still delighted in making Bernardo's stomach turn.

Rather than lashing out, Bernardo had simply turned away and walked on to his room. Behind him, Anthony had called out mockingly, 'Good to see you, Pedro. Shame you never grew a pair.'

So, as he'd just explained to the police, he had perhaps wanted to kill Anthony Pritchard. But he hadn't. And he almost felt ashamed that he hadn't had the guts to do it. Instead, Bernardo had sat in his hotel room alone and cried. The wine had helped a little. Michael Winterbottom had helped a lot. The kind-hearted manager had brought him up his favourite supper without him even having to order it. He'd said he had realised something was off when he'd spotted Bernardo in the foyer earlier.

'So, you see, officers,' Bernardo had explained, 'the only reason that Michael Winterbottom came up to the third floor was to bring me a tray of food. He had nothing to do with what went on in Room 304. He's an innocent man, I'm telling you now.'

Of course, Bernardo knew that he was probably now the prime suspect in this case. He had told the police everything. They knew that he hadn't been on stage that night; they were aware that he had consumed a great deal of wine in his room; he'd filled them in on the bullying. If he was a detective looking into this murder, he'd probably have arrested himself by now.

Admittedly, Bernardo had decided not to mention that the Valentine's evening had eventually become a complete blur. He really couldn't remember much about the second half of the evening. But the police had enough to go on already, he'd decided. And he also hadn't shared with them the fact that he'd done some hard thinking in the early part of that fateful evening.

85

Bernardo loved the acting world. He got such a thrill from being on stage. He'd got to travel a lot and he'd met the most amazing people. But Spain was where his heart lay. It always had. He had felt its pull more and more in recent years. He was still young enough to start afresh, to set up that little bed and breakfast place he'd been dreaming of for quite some time. He had no emotional ties in England now. He was a single agent. Not of his own choosing. But there it was.

But was he going to have to do it all as a fugitive now, on the run from the British police, he wondered? That certainly wasn't part of the plan. But it wasn't an option he was going to rule out. Let's face it, he reflected defeatedly, he wouldn't exactly be the first person to have done it.

A gentle knock on the door of his room jolted Bernardo out of his reverie. 'Room Service,' came a voice from outside. He smiled. Michael was back.

Chapter Twenty-Nine

Sarah Johnson heard the keys turn in her large front door. She listened as it creaked open and then gently closed. She waited as footsteps padded across her hallway and a figure appeared in the doorway to the kitchen.

'Luciana,' she said from where she sat.

Luciana's shoulders slumped forward, her whole body starting to heave with sobs.

'How did it go?' asked Sarah.

'They think I killed him. I'm sure of it.' Luciana could barely speak.

'Was no one else seen going up there after you? You'd left the place by seven o'clock.'

'Well, it turns out that the member of staff seen in the lift after me just slipped something under Anthony's door. He wouldn't have known if he was dead or alive at that stage.'

'Oh Luciana. What a mess. I can't believe you were there that evening. And I can't believe you got yourself picked up on camera. You didn't think to use the stairs? They don't have cameras on the emergency exits.'

Luciana raised her tear-stained face and stared at Sarah for a moment.

'So, what did you tell the police?' Sarah continued, ignoring Luciana's questioning eyes.

'Pretty much what I told you. How Anthony had started taking a bit of an interest in me. How I'd felt flattered that such a handsome man would even notice me. How he'd suggested that we could have some time together now and again. How I was lonely and homesick, and completely out of my depth once it had all started. How I'd only met him once before that evening. How I'd realised how seedy and second-rate the whole thing was after seeing the beautiful bouquet of roses he'd given you that morning before he'd left for work. How we'd argued, and how I'd stormed out soon after I'd arrived.'

Tears streamed down Luciana's face. 'Sarah, I am so, so sorry about this. I just seemed to fall under his spell.'

'Luciana, you're not the first to fall for Anthony's charms. I understand completely. Come here, sweetie.' Sarah opened her arms and pulled the frightened young girl into her embrace. She gazed across at the wedding photograph on the wall near her. Her eyes bore nothing but disdain.

Chapter Thirty

February 23

Perched on a desk in the station office, DI Sloane scanned the bank statements in his hand. He frowned. The sporadic cash payments into Anthony Pritchard's account were interesting. They already knew that he'd been blackmailing Michael Winterbottom. But Anthony's bank statements seemed to suggest that his demands were a little more widespread than that. Had this man created a nice side line in extortion? He shook his head. The more he learnt about the murder victim, the less surprised he became that he'd been murdered.

He wasn't at all convinced that the young au pair had done it. She didn't seem to have a strong enough motive. Would you stab someone to death for buying you a cheap box of chocolates? And she had left the hotel room within fifteen minutes. Their argument would have had to have escalated pretty quickly.

They also now had Michael Winterbottom's updated statement that he had only slipped the envelope under the door and hadn't even entered the room. How would the envelope have got over to the other side of the room if Anthony was already dead?

They'd had another chat with Sophie Hawkins, and had drawn a blank there really. She'd claimed that she hadn't mentioned Fabian because she didn't think it would cast her in a good light, after the way he'd left so suddenly. She'd explained to them that she found it a little suffocating being back home after her travels and that she was trying to establish some sort of independence from her parents by working a little further afield. The Language School in Lower Haddelton had spoken very highly of her. There really didn't seem to be any red flags there for now, as Thorne had pointed out several times on the way back to the station.

Sloane turned to Thorne at the desk next to him. At times, his young colleague seemed almost like a shadow of his former self. He'd lost some of that spark that had won the Inspector over when they'd first worked together. Sloane knew what it was like to lose the love of your life. He could feel his pain. He watched Thorne as he sat slouched in front of a computer, his eyes fixed half-heartedly on the screen.

'How's it all going?' Sloane asked.

'I'm just going through the CCTV footage that has been passed on to us from some of the shops near Lottan Lodge. You never know, there might have been some suspicious activity in the vicinity.'

'Well done. But I meant how's it going outside of work? The Emily situation?'

Thorne's eyes clouded over. 'Oh. Well, I did find out that she was in Brighton for a hen weekend. One of her best friends is getting married soon. In fact, most of them seem to be, if they haven't already.' He sighed.

'How old is Emily?'

'She turned thirty in November.'

'Right. A big birthday. What did you get her?'

'A coat.'

'A coat?'

'Yes, she'd been saying how cold it was getting and how her old coat was quite thin. I thought I'd get her something really useful.'

'What about Christmas? What did you get her then?'

'A power drill.'

'A power drill?'

'Yes, she'd been going on about how she wanted to put up some shelves in her flat. I always tried to put some thought into her presents. And it was a really good drill. Cost quite a bit.'

'Did Emily have any idea that you were thinking of proposing? Did she know that you were looking for a ring?'

'No. I'd been teasing her actually. I'd been saying that I was looking at hoovers as her Valentine's Day present. Her hoover was on the blink.'

'Harry,' Sloane said gently, 'if I were you, I'd gamble on one last sweeping gesture. Buy that ring, meet up with Emily, get down on one knee. You might be pleasantly surprised by her reaction.'

'D'you think? I'm not so sure.'

'Harry, life's too short for any sort of procrastination. Believe me, I know. I have no regrets at marrying Helen so young. Thank goodness I did. And what have you got to lose anyway?'

'My dignity,' Harry laughed.

'You'll still be dignified, whatever happens. But at least you'll have tried. And if you don't ask, the answer is always no.'

Thorne turned to the computer in front of him and fixed his eyes back on the screen. But those eyes had come alive. They were sharp and alert again. They smiled even.

Sloane called across to McArdle, 'Any updates for me?'

'Well, we spoke to various members of staff again when we were over at the hotel yesterday. George Henderson, the Manager, is clearly feeling the strain of all of this, and is very keen for us to get it all wrapped up. He's obviously in shock about it all, and just wants to put this whole incident behind them as quickly as possible. A murdered hotel guest is not good for business. We have plenty of evidence that he was nowhere near Lottan Lodge on the night of the murder, so we're not really treating him as a suspect as things stand.' McArdle brought his notes over to where Sloane was sitting.

'We spoke at length to Dolores Gonzalez. She does like to chat, doesn't she? We managed to broach the subject of her late daughter. And she did choke up a little at one point. Apparently, the girl went a little off the rails when they all moved over from Colombia. Her daughter was fifteen at the time and found it hard to settle down. She wasn't at the same school as Anthony Pritchard and Bernardo Castillo. They got her into a girls' school just outside Lower Haddelton. And Dolores claims to have never crossed paths with either of the men before. She was aware of Anthony Pritchard, or Anthony Smith as she knew him, spending occasional evenings at the hotel over the last few months. She had also noticed various young girls slipping in and out of his room. She confirmed that she'd briefly spoken to Luciana Alvarez, the au pair, on one occasion. But merely to direct her towards the lifts. She'd asked the girl if she was from Colombia, but Luciana had seemed reluctant to engage in any sort of conversation with her. Probably wise,' McArdle laughed.

'What did she say about her daughter's death?' asked Sloane.

'So, the daughter became a bit of a wild child by all accounts. She was hanging around with the wrong crowd, that sort of thing. Dolores and her husband had thought that a trip back to Colombia would somehow help. They couldn't have been more wrong. All the partying seems to have spiralled out of control over there, and she appears to have ended up choking on her own vomit after a particularly heavy night. They never saw her alive again. Tragic really.'

'Yes, horrible. Is there any connection to Anthony Pritchard anywhere at all? I'd quite understand her wanting to stab him to death if there were.'

'No, there isn't. We haven't uncovered anything at all to link Dolores or her family to the victim. And, allegedly, Dolores was down on the ground floor for most of the evening. Apart from a couple of visits up to the first floor with room service. The kitchen staff both swear that she was in with them most of the time, sitting on a stool and chatting. We've managed to retrieve some footage from the hotel restaurant. Dolores is seen moving in and out of the area at times. Michael Winterbottom and Sophie Hawkins are also seen talking in the deserted restaurant shortly before eight o'clock.'

'Sir,' came Thorne's voice suddenly. 'Have a look at this. This is from outside a supermarket just round the corner from Lottan Lodge at twenty-five to eight on the night of the murder. Guess who we've got on camera walking towards the hotel?'

Sloane peered towards the screen and raised his eyebrows. The footage was somewhat grainy, but a tall blonde woman in a pale-coloured coat could be clearly seen, striding in the direction of Lottan Lodge. 'That's Sarah Johnson,' he said, struggling to keep the excitement out of his voice.

'Yes. And look who's with her.'

Sloane narrowed his eyes. Less distinct in the dark sweatshirt and leggings that she wore, a second figure soon became visible under the light of the street lamp she passed. 'Well, I never. Arabella Winthorpe-Holmes.'

'Two angry women. Two stab wounds. Talk about putting two and two together.' Thorne laughed.

'Right, I want them both in for questioning. These two women have been running rings around us. They have clearly become acquainted somehow or other, and they must have worked out what Anthony was up to.'

'D'you know what?' said Thorne, 'This is starting to remind me of that film where it turns out that they've all queued up to stab the victim. Are we sure that Forensics didn't miss a few puncture wounds? By the sounds of it, there could have been at least half a dozen people lined up in that hotel corridor, waiting for their turn.'

'Well, for now, let's see if these two had anything to do with it. We need to get them in as soon as they realise that we are onto them. We don't want to give them any time to brush up on their stories. And we'll interview them separately, of course. This is going to be very interesting.'

Chapter Thirty-One

February 24

Behind the reception desk at Lottan Lodge, Sophie wearily replaced the telephone receiver and double-checked that she'd entered the booking onto the system. She really didn't know how much longer she could do this. In fact, she was starting to wonder if there was a point to it any more. Was she ever going to see this all through? She knew that she'd pretty much lost her nerve by now.

Admittedly, she was finally getting the hang of things as far as the job was concerned. Even Michael Winterbottom had smiled at her this morning. He seemed to be smiling a lot these last couple of days. Which seemed a bit odd, as they were all being treated as potential murderers by the police at the moment.

Sophie had been a little jittery after that last conversation with those two detectives. Despite the fact that the younger one had seemed to be almost flirting with her, the older one definitely suspected something. She was sure of it. Though she wasn't certain as to which of them had made her feel more uncomfortable. The young sergeant had seemed harmless enough, but it had almost felt weirdly like speed dating when he was talking. The way he kept asking her about her interests and trying too hard to crack jokes. Sorry, she thought, but if she was online, she'd have swiped left. He just wasn't her type.

Unlike the person who had just come through the hotel doors into the foyer and stood silhouetted against the pale spring sunshine outside. His large, battered rucksack was slung over one shoulder, his hair neck-length and tousled. The loose-fitting, creased clothes did nothing to disguise his athletic figure. The dark beard failed to conceal his adorable smile.

'Fabian!' Sophie cried, as she watched him draw slowly nearer. She couldn't believe her eyes. It felt almost like a dream.

When he eventually reached her, he allowed his bag to slip to the ground, took both her hands, and asked, 'Have you done it yet?'

Sophie, feeling the reassuring strength of his fingers, replied simply, 'Tonight. I'm going to do it tonight.'

Chapter Thirty-Two

Sarah Johnson's mobile phone rang, as she knew it would. Not her big shiny new phone, of course. It was her cheap pay-as-you-go one. Anthony wasn't the only person capable of a little subterfuge.

'Hello,' she said, as she put the phone calmly to her ear.

'Have they contacted you?' came the anxious voice. 'We've been rumbled.'

'Arabella. It's fine. Don't panic. They can't pin anything on us.'

'But they've got us on camera, heading for the hotel.'

'That doesn't prove anything. My lawyer is meeting me at the station. And his associate will sit in with you.'

'Are you sure? I'll be able to pay you back once my money comes through. Thank you so much. Sarah, I'm terrified.'

'Don't be. Everything is going to be absolutely fine.'

'So, we stick to our story? You know they're going to separate us when they do the interview?'

'It'll be fine. However, there is one thing that I need you to say. And I'll say it too. It's quite important.'

'Okay. What is it?'

'Well, you won't believe this, but Luciana was caught on camera at the hotel that evening.'

'What? My God, it gets worse. Was there nothing that man wasn't capable of?'

'Indeed. Anyway, she's now a suspect, of course. Poor girl. The thing is, I don't want her getting arrested and punished for this crime. We both know that Anthony deserved everything he got that night.'

'So, what do you want me to say?'

'We need to cover for her. Tell the police that when we knocked on Anthony's door that evening, we heard movement in the bathroom, but he didn't hear us and didn't answer. That would prove that Luciana couldn't have done it. She had left the hotel long before we got there. And don't forget to mention that we heard a noise further up the corridor.'

'Fine. It's more or less true. He didn't answer the door to us.'

'Exactly. Someone seems to have got to him before us. He was clearly already dead when we were knocking on that door. He loved a good fight, did Anthony. He wouldn't have been able to resist if he'd heard our voices.'

'Sarah! We weren't actually going to kill him.'

'Who knows, Arabella, who knows?' Sarah laughed.

'You're terrible, Sarah! Anyway, good luck. We'll talk afterwards and compare notes. I hope I don't cock this up.'

'You'll be absolutely fine. Just stick to our story. We'll have those detectives in the palm of our hands, you'll see.'

'I really hope so. I feel like I'm about to go on stage. I've literally got stage fright.'

'Arabella, I have no doubt that yours will be an Oscar-worthy performance. You'll be fabulous, my darling. Now off you go. Your audience awaits.'

Out of habit, Sarah placed the phone carefully back into the empty cake tin it had lived in for the past three months. Anthony would never have thought to look there – she had never baked a cake in her life. As she stood there in the silence, with a satisfied expression on her perfectly made-up face, her gaze travelled across to the family photographs on the nearby wall. She smiled triumphantly.

Chapter Thirty-Three

In the larger of the two interview rooms, DI Sloane looked across the table at Sarah Johnson.

'Would you like to take your coat off, Mrs Pritchard? It's quite warm in here. You can lay it on that chair in the corner if you like.'

'Not yet. And by the way, it's Ms Johnson. I think I've already made that clear. But call me Sarah, of course.'

Sarah stood up and held her arms out wide.

Sloane glanced at Sarah's lawyer, sitting quietly next to her. He remained unperturbed. Clearly, he knew what this was all about.

'Inspector, take a good look, please.'

Sloane did what he was told.

'Do you recognise this coat?'

And then it dawned on him. This was the coat that Sarah had been wearing the night of the murder. It was a pale, camel coloured woollen coat. Clearly very expensive. Clearly devoid of blood stains.

'Inspector, I know what you think. And I know what it looks like. But, before you start, I would like to make it very clear that if I had been planning to stab my husband to death, I would most certainly not have worn my best woollen coat.' Sarah nodded towards the tape recorder. 'For the record, can you confirm that you can see no blood on my coat?'

'Sarah, take a seat please,' said Sloane uncomfortably. 'We will ask Forensics to take a look at your coat, of course. Let's just start at the beginning, shall we?'

He cleared his throat. 'So, when did you realise that Anthony was living this double life?'

'About three months ago,' said Arabella to Thorne, in the smaller interview room next door.

'And how did you find out?' asked Thorne.

'It was all because of a chance encounter in the A&E department at the hospital in Lower Haddelton. It's the nearest hospital for both of us. Even though we both live about twenty minutes away in different directions. I was there one evening with Henry, and Sarah was there with Olly. We had to wait for ages, of course. Olly had a suspected broken arm, and Henry had a funny rash. Both were false alarms in the end, by the way. Anyway, we got chatting. About our sons, our jobs, our homes. And the man in our lives.'

'Of course, it didn't take us long to work out that it was the very same man. And that we were taking turns,' said Sarah. Sloane was all ears by now.

'Had you suspected anything before then?' he asked.

'Nothing,' said Sarah. 'I feel so foolish. I was madly in love with him. Everything I've told you was true up until three months ago.'

'I had absolutely no idea,' said Arabella. 'I adored him. I was about to shower him with the proceeds of my trust fund.'

Thorne was scribbling in his notepad like never before.

'So why did you wait three months?' he asked, looking up briefly.

'Well,' said Sarah, 'we decided to buy some pay-as-you-go phones that day, and stay in touch. We wanted to plan our next move carefully. But before too long, we realised that Anthony was spending the odd night away from both of us. I eventually came across a couple of receipts for drinks purchased at Lottan Lodge. Very sloppy of him really. Anyway, we worked out where he was going. We just didn't know who with.'

Sloane caught Sarah's eye. 'Sarah, why did you and Arabella visit Lottan Lodge on the evening of the fourteenth of February?'

'We wanted to catch him out,' said Arabella. 'Neither of us could stand the sight of him by then. Sarah was planning to tell him that she was divorcing him, and I was going to throw my pathetic engagement ring back at him. We wanted to do it together. We wanted to see his face when he realised that we knew each other.'

'Did you end up killing Anthony?' asked Thorne.

'Absolutely not. We both have a young child who relies on us,' said Arabella.

'Absolutely not,' said Sarah. 'I've told you, I was wearing my best coat.'

'So, how did you get up to the room?' asked Sloane.

'We used the stairs. But only because we didn't want to run the risk of bumping into Anthony on the way up. As I've said, we had no intention of killing him and had no reason to hide.'

'How did you know which room he was in?'

'I just asked the young girl on reception. Said I'd been nearby with my friend and I wanted to surprise my husband, Anthony, as it was Valentine's Day. Don't get her sacked though. I was very convincing. The poor girl didn't stand a chance.'

'And what happened when you knocked on his door?'

'Not a lot really,' said Arabella. 'We knocked a couple of times, as we could hear movement in the bathroom. But he obviously couldn't hear us. He certainly didn't come to the door. But he was definitely there, moving around. Maybe he'd put earphones in?'

'How long were you there for?' asked Thorne.

'Only about five minutes. Until about ten to eight, I'd say. That's when we heard the loud noise from further up the corridor.'

'A loud noise?' repeated Sloane.

'Yes. From a nearby room, up nearer the lifts.'

'What sort of noise?'

'It was a clanging noise, I suppose. It was only for a moment. But it was enough to scare us. We knew that we shouldn't have been there really. And Anthony wasn't playing ball. So, we made a run for it, back down the stairs. Ten minutes later, I was ordering my first cocktail, and Arabella was through the turnstile at her gym. But I'm sure you've clarified all that by now.'

Sloane nodded. 'So, can I just confirm that, as far as you know, Anthony Pritchard was still alive at ten minutes to eight?'

'Absolutely. And I know for a fact that Luciana was back home with Olly at that time. I would never have left my son on his own.'

'And do you believe that someone else could possibly have been on that third-floor corridor as you left the scene with Arabella?'

'Yes, I do,' said Sarah with practised certainty. 'There was definitely someone else up there.'

She looked Sloane confidently in the eye. 'Inspector, if you can establish who that was, I think you'll have found your murderer.'

Chapter Thirty-Four

Dolores clambered slowly up the few concrete steps leading to a large metal door. The door was sturdy and secure, and she struggled a little to turn its stiff handle. Only by using her shoulder did she manage to ease it slowly open. She shivered as she stepped outside onto the sprawling expanse of concrete; the rooftop of Lottan Lodge. A gust of wind caught a discarded paper cup and dragged an empty cigarette packet erratically around. Unlit, the dim terrace relied on the clear night sky above to cast an indistinct glow on its bleak landscape. The blanket of stars, blinking down at the darkness up there, did very little to brighten the gloom. A broken bottle just about glinted in the hazy moonlight.

Dolores pulled her cardigan tightly together and headed towards the faint glow that came from beyond the low, concrete edge of the rooftop. She'd always loved coming up here after a long shift. The hotel got so hot and stuffy. It was the perfect way to clear her head. Nobody else seemed to even be aware of this little hideaway. She'd certainly never bumped into anyone else up here since she'd discovered it. In fact, she imagined that it was probably completely out of bounds. She always felt a little giddy when she dared to peer over the edge at the world going on far beneath her. Lower Haddelton looked so different from these lofty heights.

A low hum of traffic rose up to meet Dolores as she stood and breathed in the cold night air, staring out at the town, now bathed in the glare of orange street lights. Occasionally, muffled voices floated up, and the odd shriek of laughter echoed off the nearby buildings. To one side of her, the river stretched out, with stark, bare trees swaying on the opposite riverbank. Its bridge was lit up in a diaphanous blue, reflecting perfectly in the dark water beneath it. Tiny, distant strings of fairy lights swung precariously outside the riverside restaurants, fragile in the unrelenting breeze.

A loud grating sound from behind her made Dolores jump. She steadied herself on the cold concrete ledge in front of her.

Slowly, she turned, her eyes adjusting gradually to the gloomy shadows of the remote rooftop.

'Sophie?' she said.

Chapter Thirty-Five

Dolores watched uncertainly as the vague, obscured figure drew close and took shape. The moonlight shone down eerily on the haunted face that revealed itself, the wide, dark eyes contrasting with the girl's ghostly pallor. Her long black hair had come loose and flew wildly around in the wind. She was shaking.

'Sophie?' Dolores said again. She was close enough to see the terrified look on the girl's face.

'Dolores, I'm so sorry. I've thought long and hard about whether I should do this. I nearly walked away from it all earlier today. I'd decided I should just go back to my cosy little life, see a bit more of the world, just be grateful for everything I already have. This whole situation seems to have spiralled out of control so quickly.'

'Sophie, you don't have to do anything you don't want to, you know?' Dolores glanced towards the large metal door behind Sophie on the other side of the rooftop.'

'It's not that I don't want to do it. It's just that I'm scared.'

'You want to do it?'

'Yes. But part of me still thinks that it would be better all round just to leave it.'

'Sophie, has someone else put you up to this?'

'Sort of, I suppose.'

'Think of your family, Sophie. Think how your actions could have consequences for them. How would they feel about all of this?'

'That's just it. I don't want to upset them.'

'Do you have a happy family life, Sophie?'

'I do. I really do. I've got the best mum and dad in the world. It's just that... I'm adopted.'

Dolores stared at the tense young girl in front of her for a moment. She took in her large almond-shaped brown eyes; her oval face and high cheekbones; the slight dimple in her chin; her sleek dark hair blowing around in the wind. And then she understood. It all at once became so clear. How could she not have realised?

'Sofia?' Dolores said shakily. Her heart began to race. She felt almost light-headed.

'Dolores, do you know my birth mother? Are we related somehow?'

Sophie continued looking at Dolores warily. 'All I know is that I was named Sofia Dolores at birth and that I was born in Lower Haddelton hospital.'

Her words started to tumble out. 'I'd never really given too much thought to finding my birth mother, as I'd had such a happy childhood. Then, when I travelled through Colombia, so many people asked me if I had Colombian family. Everyone was so lovely. I suppose it got me thinking. I decided to do a bit of investigating for myself and managed to get a teaching job over this way so I could spend more time in Lower Haddelton. I couldn't believe it when Fabian started talking about a Colombian lady called Dolores who worked at his hotel. We hatched this plan that he would suddenly take off, leaving the hotel in the lurch, and then I'd contact them, asking about a job, just happening to be in the right place at the right time. Fabian had been thinking about doing a bit of travelling around the UK and was more than happy to be moving on from Lottan Lodge.

He was really supportive about me looking into my family background, whereas I had huge doubts about approaching you. I was so scared about ruining people's lives. I've tried to pluck up the courage to speak to you so many times, but I just never seemed to manage to go through with it. Then, of course, Fabian disappeared off the face of the earth, so I had no one to encourage me. I was starting to lose my nerve really. He's back now by the way, I don't know if you heard. He spent a couple of weeks at a retreat on some remote Scottish island, but left because he was missing me.'

Sophie raised her eyes, guarded and hesitant. 'So, do you know her? My mother.'

Dolores' eyes filled with tears. 'Sofia, I did know her. Your mother was a light who shone too brightly for this world.'

'Was? What do you mean 'was'?'

'Your wonderful mother was taken from us when she was even younger than you. She was my darling daughter, and the most beautiful person to walk this earth. I miss her every single day of my life.'

Dolores wiped her eyes. 'You know, she was only seventeen when she had you. Just a child herself. Giving you away for adoption was one of the hardest things that I've ever had to do. We had no money back then, and, of course, we thought Elena had her whole life in front of her.'

'So, my mother's dead? I've gone through all this soul-searching, all this effort to track her down, and she's dead?' Sophie started to sob.

Dolores stepped forward and swept up the shivering, broken girl into her arms.

'Come here, *niñita*,' she said. 'It may be a small consolation, but you have a grandmother now. A grandmother with a big heart full of love; love that has had nowhere to go for an awfully long time.'

Sophie managed a weak smile. 'Dolores, will you tell me all about her? My mother.'

'Of course I will. And it's grandma, or *abuelita,* from now on, if you'd like.' Dolores said gently.

'*Suena bien,*' replied Sophie shyly, and returned her grandmother's embrace.

Chapter Thirty-Six

FOUR WEEKS LATER

March 24

Dolores had nearly reached the doorway that led down to the hotel's underground car park when she heard Michael Winterbottom calling her name. Her heart sank. What had she done now, she wondered? She'd been there since the crack of dawn and all she really wanted to do was get home. She had a whole free afternoon stretching out in front of her and she was determined to make the most of it.

'Dolores, have you got a moment?' Michael called again.

Dolores turned wearily to meet her fate. Yet Michael, behind the reception desk, appeared to be wringing his hands with excitement.

'Dolores, hurry up. I've got so much to fill you in on,' he said, almost in a stage whisper.

Dolores raised her eyebrows. Well, this was unexpected.

'I've just been in with George,' Michael said, as she got close enough for confidences to be shared. 'Firstly, I wanted to let you know that I've given my notice in.'

'Oh Michael, that's a shame. We're all going to miss you,' Dolores lied pleasantly.

'The thing is, Dolores, I've been very unhappy these last few months. In fact, I've been extremely miserable, and I know I haven't been the most pleasant person to be around. So, I'm sorry if my behaviour has affected your working life. I'm sure you'll be glad to see the back of me really.'

Dolores' eyes softened. 'The place won't be the same without you Michael. You run a very tight ship.'

'Why, thank you Dolores. And you are a credit to the hotel too. In your own way.'

Dolores laughed. 'So, where are you off to? Do you have a new job lined up?'

'Well, you might be quite surprised to hear this, but I'm off to Spain. I'm going to be involved in the running of a little bed and breakfast place on the Costa del Sol.'

Dolores watched as Michael's face turned pink. He was blushing, she thought. Yes, he was definitely blushing.

Michael went on. 'Oh, Dolores, it sounds wonderful. Seville and Granada are not too far away, and then there's the Sierra Nevada for skiing and hiking. And the beautiful coastline, of course.'

'Do you speak any Spanish, Michael?' Dolores asked, not unkindly.

'*Un poco,*' Michael said. 'But I'll be running the place with a Spanish friend. He knows the language and the culture, and I know the hospitality business. We're the perfect combination really.'

'Well, that's wonderful news. I'm very happy for you. What did George say?'

Michael peered over his shoulder. 'Actually, don't let anyone else know as yet, but George is leaving too. It would appear that there's a new management team coming in to take over the running of this place. They're going to throw a bit of money at it, spruce it up a bit, I think. George is more than happy about it all. I think he just wants to be on a golf course these days. Did you hear that Sophie has given her notice in too?'

'Really?' said Dolores grinning. 'Well, there's a big old world out there for her to discover while she's still young.'

'Yes, apparently, she's heading off to Paris to teach English. From what I understand, she hooked up with Fabian when he turned up again out of the blue. That took me by surprise a little, I must say. You can never tell, can you? I'd considered a bit of a jaunt out to Paris myself at one point. But I suppose it wasn't to be.'

'The weather will be much nicer in Spain, Michael,' smiled Dolores.

'Yes. And I am so grateful to Fabian for the great character reference he gave to the police about me. There had been a little misunderstanding at one point – I won't bore you with the details - but whatever he said seems to have done the trick. I think the police crossed me off their list of suspects there and then.'

'Well, it sounds like we're all pretty much off the hook. They seem to have found enough footage of us to satisfy their curiosity. Though there are huge gaps in the CCTV coverage. It must have been so difficult for those detectives to build any kind of case.'

'Yes, George just told me that the police think some shady associate of Anthony Pritchard managed to sneak in undetected. They believe that there might have been a bit of drug dealing, or something like that, going on. Though what baffles me is how the person got hold of a steak knife.'

'Good point. Perhaps they'd sneaked it out on a previous visit?'

'Who knows? Anyway, they are keeping the case open for now. But the staff and the guests are no longer being treated as suspects.'

'That's good to hear,' laughed Dolores.

'So, what about you, Dolores? Any plans for retirement, if you don't mind me asking?'

'Good question, Michael. I think I'm going to stay on for a little while yet. Show these young whippersnappers that come in how it should be done.' She smiled.

'Dolores, I hope my Spanish will be as good as your English one day.'

'*Gracias*, Michael.'

'Now you get off. Enjoy your free afternoon.'

'I will. *Adiós*.'

'*Adiós*, Dolores.'

As Dolores reached the door to the car park, she could hear Michael contentedly humming. She beamed. Yes, it was all very unexpected.

Chapter Thirty-Seven

Sarah put down her phone and gazed out into her garden. Spring was in the air, bringing its promise of new life. Lovingly planted daffodils danced playfully along the neat borders, silken heads of striking yellow jostling in the breeze. Strategically positioned crocuses emerged amongst them, a deep, sumptuous purple. The large, carefully pruned camellia in one corner of the large garden had blossomed, and huge crimson blooms now covered it. Next to it, a blanket of pale petals lay beneath the thriving magnolia tree, her pride and joy. The golden forsythia in another corner, flawlessly trimmed, dazzled in the pale sunshine. Only occasional high clouds scudded across the pastel blue sky. The days were longer now. All around, buds were set to unfurl, and bright fledgling leaves appeared as if from nowhere. Her lawn was becoming lush and unruly, the grass awakening and stretching after its winter slumber. She smiled proudly. Though her gardener would have his work cut out before too long, she thought.

Sarah turned as the knock on her front door echoed across the hallway of her silent house. Her soft sheepskin slippers barely made a sound as she calmly rose from where she sat and made her way across the room.

'Nice house,' came the voice, as she pulled open the door.

Sarah laughed. 'And it's all mine now. Well, it was always mine really. I've been the one paying for it all this time.' She grinned. 'Still, looks like Anthony had a great life insurance policy in place. One of the perks of his job, I suppose. The mortgage is going to be paid off in full, and a nice lump sum will be winging its way to my bank account before too long. Once those very nice policemen confirm that I couldn't possibly have killed my gorgeous, but rather shady, husband off. Fortunately, it seems that Anthony had his finger in far too many pies not to have made some pretty serious enemies. People with bigger grievances to settle than a woman scorned evidently.

She pulled the door open wide, smiling. 'Or two women scorned, maybe. Come on in. It's lovely to see you again in person. You look well. Your hair's grown since the last time I saw you.'

'Yours hasn't,' laughed Arabella. 'Have you just stepped out of a hairdresser's? You look just as fabulous as ever.'

'Thank you. It's because of my job really. I certainly hadn't been trying to impress Anthony these last few months.'

Sarah took in the dainty young woman in her hallway in her ancient, over-sized waxed jacket, with a silk equestrian scarf tied at her neck. She wore a floral Alice band to hold back her long, wavy hair. Well, thought Sarah, you can take the girl out of the Home Counties, but there was no taking the Home Counties out of this girl, elopement to the South London suburbs or not. Her gaze travelled down to the grubby boots that Arabella's well-worn jeans were tucked into.

'Don't worry,' Arabella laughed, looking around. 'I'll take them off.'

'Thank you,' Sarah smiled. 'Then come on through. I'll make you a cup of tea. We have the place to ourselves. Olly is at school, and Luciana's out with a friend.'

'Oh dear. We all know what happened the last time she said she'd made a friend,' said Arabella, as she followed Sarah through to the kitchen.

'No, it's okay. I've met her. It's another au pair. She's from Brazil.'

'So what's Luciana going to do now? Will you keep her on?'

'Yes, for a while longer. I spoke to her agency and we've put her in touch with a few other girls doing the same thing. I hadn't realised how lonely she'd been. She's a sweet little thing really. And she's so good with Olly. I don't want to lose her quite yet. Even after everything that has happened.'

'And how is Olly doing? He must be so confused.'

'Yes. That was a very hard conversation. Olly idolised his father. And for all his faults, Anthony was actually quite a good dad. Well, when he was around. It was possibly the only thing that he got right in the grubby little life that he led. I've told Olly that Anthony got killed while he was fighting off baddies. Of course, I'm a bit worried that he's going to see him as some kind

111

of war hero now, but then maybe that's the kindest way for him to deal with it for the time being.' Sarah reached up for some mugs. 'How about Henry?'

'I don't think he's even noticed, thank goodness. Annoyingly, the only word that he's started saying recently is dada. But I know not to read too much into that. Supposedly, it's just a very easy word for a baby to master. Well, that's what I'm telling myself.' She laughed. 'I have to say, Anthony was very sweet with Henry too. But then I guess it's very easy to coo over a baby when you're only doing it part-time. Henry won't even remember him, of course. And I'm glad. Anthony wouldn't have exactly been a positive male role-model for a young boy, would he?'

Arabella glanced around the flawless room. 'This place is so beautiful, Sarah. God knows how Anthony put up with living in that rented house with me.'

'He obviously had a very good idea about what was coming, didn't he? He was playing the long game. Anthony knew exactly what he was doing.'

'You know, it still hurts. Even after everything that's happened, everything that I know now. I still can't believe what he did, and how he got away with it for so long. I met Anthony two and a half years ago. For all that time he managed to live this double life, hedging his bets, working out how to achieve the maximum return on his assets. Us two. I often wonder if he ever really loved me. Or had he already done his due diligence before he stepped into my life? I feel so foolish.'

'I'm sure he had feelings for you, Arabella. No matter how mercenary Anthony was, he wouldn't have gone about setting up a life with you if he didn't love you.' Sarah busied herself with the teabags to hide the doubt in her eyes.

'What about you, Sarah? Do you feel that yours was a genuine marriage? Perhaps Anthony was just someone who was capable of loving two different people at the same time?'

'He certainly swept me off my feet when I first met him. I'd been so busy concentrating on my career, I hadn't given much time or effort to my love life. It all seemed a bit too good to be true really. He was the missing piece of the jigsaw and he just slotted in perfectly. Anthony was never going to be the breadwinner, but he brought so much else to the table. He

112

certainly ticked more than enough boxes. He was attractive, charming and funny. And, of course, I'd decided that I wanted to be a mother by then.' Sarah paused.

'Did he love me? I certainly believe that he thought he loved me at first. But, in the end, he loved money more than he loved me. You know, I never signed a pre-nuptial agreement. How stupid was that? He would have got half of everything if he'd gone through with his very likely plans to divorce me and enjoy the spoils of your trust fund.' She sighed defeatedly.

'Well, he got his comeuppance in the end, didn't he?' smiled Arabella, her eyes hardening suddenly. She took a determined sip of her tea. 'Now, my money comes through in a couple of weeks. We've got a holiday to plan.'

'Absolutely. And I want you to have half of whatever money comes through from Anthony's insurance policy. He doesn't seem to have written a will. But you deserve the money just as much as me.'

'I think I'm going to have more money than I'll know how to spend, so don't you worry about me.'

'So where do you fancy going?'

Arabella grinned widely. 'I thought the Caribbean might be nice. The boys would love it.'

'Great idea. Whereabouts?'

'So many islands, so little time. We might have to go every year.'

The sunlight caught the two women's mugs of tea as they raised them aloft to seal their pact.

'To us,' they said, and laughed.

113

Chapter Thirty-Eight

DI Sloane checked his satnav before indicating, and slowly turned out of the remote industrial estate that, as it transpired, was not the scene of a brutal murder.

'Well, that was a waste of time,' said DS Thorne.

'I suppose you never know. It must have been a bit of a shock for that young chap to spot an unmoving human arm emerging from a large container.'

'He needs to get his eyes checked if you ask me. And did he not think to go round the front of the warehouse to see what sort of business was going on there? If you're making wedding dresses and the like, you're going to need the odd mannequin or two.'

'I know. But it was very lifelike, you must admit. Don't you always say that appearances can be deceptive? It's one of your catchphrases, isn't it?' Sloane smiled.

'I wouldn't mind, but we've come so far out. This place is miles from Haddelton. I don't know why someone a bit closer couldn't have attended the scene.'

'We're the best in the business, clearly,' laughed Sloane.

'Obviously,' said Thorne, grinning. 'Except we haven't worked out who killed Anthony Pritchard yet.'

'I think our victim was caught up in a murky world. From what that Mexican girl said the other day to McArdle, it sounds like he could have been grooming young girls. He seems to have been hanging around Salsa bars, picking them up there, and offering them free trips back home to South America in return for smuggling back a few drugs.'

'Yes, he was a nasty piece of work alright. And probably knew a lot of very dodgy people. You know, those poor girls, the drugs mules, swallow the packs with the drugs in them before the flight. They take all the risk. It's a horrible way to die if it all goes wrong.'

'I know. But for people like Anthony Pritchard, it's a very lucrative business, and life goes on as normal, of course.'

'Until you get on the wrong side of someone nastier than you maybe.'

Sloane nodded. 'Or until someone decides that you're dispensable? I'd still love to know who did this. I think there's life in this case yet.'

'Whatever the reason that someone did this, I'm not sure we'll ever track them down now. These people are very clever. There's been absolutely nothing on any camera footage in the area. Whoever stabbed Anthony Pritchard to death seems to have just disappeared back into the woodwork. And for once, I don't really care.' Thorne glanced out at the unfamiliar roads.

'So, how's it going with Emily?' asked Sloane.

'Swimmingly. Thanks again for your idea about the ring. Her face when she saw it. She was over the moon. She literally couldn't stop smiling. She said that she'd been wanting to get engaged for ages, and had all but given up on me. What with me going on about hoovers and everything.'

'Have you set a date yet?'

'We're looking into it at the moment. Maybe next spring? I'll keep you posted. You're going to be one of my guests of honour. If it wasn't for you, I don't know where we'd be.'

'Did she like the ring you chose?'

'She absolutely loved it, thank goodness. I've got a few photos of it. I'll find a good one to show you.'

As Thorne leant forward, peering down cheerily at the phone in his lap, Sloane gently came to a halt at a crossing where a jogger waited. Kitted out in expensive running gear, toned and lean, bursting with health, the woman was a stark reminder that he really ought to be doing more exercise. She panted evenly at the edge of the pavement, running on the spot, unwilling to break her momentum. Looking very much the part in the smart cap pulled down over her face and the gleaming wrap-around mirrored sunglasses, the runner checked the fitness watch on her wrist as she began to pound softly across the road. She turned briefly to nod to Sloane, who watched her; a fleeting exchange of glances, very short-lived, yet enough to cause the Inspector to narrow his eyes. It was, in fact, when the jogger turned away and raised her hand to thank the other vehicle that he saw the sleek grey plait that ran down her back; that he noticed the large green emerald on her ring finger, glinting in the pale sunlight.

'That's her ring!' said Thorne.

Sloane turned to his colleague, wide-eyed, stunned.

Beside him, Thorne held his phone up, a close-up of a diamond ring in his hand. 'Can you see there are basically three diamonds? They're just set very close together.' The young man's face was a picture of contentment. After all the misery, all the pain, everything was falling into place for him. His broken heart was on the mend. And this was his moment. A moment of pure, unadulterated happiness. And Sloane certainly wasn't going to deny him that.

The Inspector leant in for a closer look. 'It's really beautiful, Harry. I can see why Emily loves it. You've obviously got great taste. Congratulations again. I couldn't be happier for you both.'

The jarring sound of the horn from the car behind made Sloane jump. And when he turned back to the steering wheel, the jogger was nowhere to be seen. It was as though she had vanished into thin air.

'You know what, Harry,' he said, after a few moments, 'I think I am going to wrap up that case at Lottan Lodge. You're probably right. I don't think we've got a cat in hell's chance of finding who actually did it. And, when all is said and done, Anthony Pritchard pretty much got what he deserved.'

'Sounds good to me. D'you fancy a nice cup of tea when we get back? I'm parched.'

Sloane smiled, and kept his eyes firmly on the road, as he smoothly set off again towards the station.

Chapter Thirty-Nine

I'd recognised him the very first time that I'd bumped into him in the foyer. He was older now, of course. He'd filled out a little, lost his boyish youth. It had been over twenty years since I'd last seen that face; those electric blue eyes, the disarming grin, that mop of curly black hair. But I'd never forgotten what he looked like. His features were etched into my brain, even as the years passed by.

He'd clicked his fingers at me, a lesser mortal, at his beck and call, existing merely to do his bidding. He'd wanted champagne and two glasses brought to his room. The cheapest we had though, he'd made that clear.

It was obvious that he was barely tolerating Michael's efforts to ingratiate himself with this handsome new guest in front of him. Nothing would be too much trouble, Michael was assuring him, almost coquettishly. Anthony had merely looked around at the unfamiliar surroundings and curled his lip in contempt.

We'd had the pleasure of his company at least once a month after that. Always just for one night. Always paid for in cash. Always under the name of Anthony Smith. At first, I'd thought he was conducting some sort of sordid affair. He didn't wear a wedding ring, but the signs were all there. Why the need for all the subterfuge otherwise? And there were always two phones being charged when I brought up Room Service.

It was only after his third or fourth visit that I noticed. Anthony Pritchard wasn't conducting an affair. The face of the girl seemed to change quite regularly, but not the type. Young, Latin American, a little unworldly. These were not romantic assignations that were taking place. Something else was going on. And I knew exactly what that was.

Coming to live in England all those years ago had been hard for us. Leaving behind family and friends, having to learn a new language, adjusting to this awful climate, it had all been such a challenge. But Juan had felt that the job offer was just too good to turn down. The money was far better than at home, and anyway, he'd said, we didn't have to stay for ever. We rented a little place in Lower Haddelton and got Elena into a lovely girls' school nearby. She was fifteen when we moved here, our only child, and the light of our lives. She had been such an easy child. Up to that point, our beautiful daughter had brought nothing but joy into our lives. Of course, I'd fretted about how it would be an upheaval for her at that age. She was too old to simply join in with playground games, but too young to confidently initiate healthy new teenage friendships. But I'd really believed that she'd weather the brief storm and would eventually thrive. Why wouldn't she? After all, she was a bubbly, attractive, intelligent young girl, who'd been showered with love all her life.

How wrong could a mother be?

Within a year of our move, Elena had seemed to have morphed into a surly, irritable stranger, who grew more and more distant as the months went by. She struggled to settle down to any school work, and Juan and I had been quite grateful when she had started going out with friends she'd made at the school. Though we never got to meet any of them. Any suggestions of them coming round were abrasively dismissed, and we were kept pretty much in the dark as to what our daughter did in her free time.

Elena's sixth form years came to a grinding halt when she glumly announced that she was pregnant. Five months pregnant. And, by the way, she hated the father of the baby and never wanted to see him again. How had we not noticed, we'd asked ourselves?

I suppose she was spending so little time with us by then. She'd started acting as though we were the enemy. As though we were to blame for everything that was wrong in her life. And maybe we were, I would think, wracked with guilt.

The final few months of the pregnancy were a more gentle, less quarrelsome time for us. I made sure that Elena ate well and took her to all her hospital appointments. When the time came, and the baby was born, I had never seen such a beautiful child. Apart from Elena, of course. In fact, she was the image of her. Elena named the baby Sofia Dolores, and we had two days with her. I hadn't believed that it was possible to cry so much until the

*day the baby was taken from us. But, then, I didn't know what lay
ahead.*

*If there had been a positive to be taken from this agonising
moment in our lives, it was that Elena had seemed to grow closer
to us again. She embraced the love that we offered her, and for
a while our lives had held such hope.*

A year later, Elena met Anthony Pritchard.

*She'd started doing a few shifts in a pub to earn a little money
while she did her Travel and Tourism course at the local college
in Lower Haddelton. We'd all thought that it was such a clever
idea to put her Spanish to good use. The pub wasn't the most
salubrious of venues and the crowd there were rather wild for my
liking. But Elena had thought they were fun. Even now, I'm still
not exactly sure when she started seeing Anthony. We were never
officially introduced or anything. He knocked for her once or
twice and we exchanged brief pleasantries.*

*He was certainly a handsome young man, I had to give him
that. But I didn't trust him. There was something I couldn't quite
get to the bottom of about him. His eyes seemed a little cold,
despite his ready smile.*

*But all I could see in Elena's eyes was love. She was clearly
besotted with him. There were a lot of late nights, and there was
far too much drinking going on. But she seemed so happy.*

*I suppose that we were a little taken by surprise when she'd
told us that she was planning a holiday to Colombia. Particularly
when she'd explained that she was travelling alone. She'd said
that Anthony was treating her, as he knew how homesick she'd
been when we'd first arrived. Juan and I were still scrimping and
saving in those days. Flights all the way back home were just not
top of our list. Accompanying her was simply not an option. We
had our doubts, but we could see how excited she was. And
wouldn't it be wonderful for her to see her old friends and her
family, we'd both thought? Still, it had seemed a little strange
that Anthony wasn't going with her.*

*And it was somewhat odd that Anthony hadn't come to the
airport to see Elena off, when it had all been his idea in the first
place. We had taken her, of course, and had waved her off
laughing and smiling. We hadn't known that it would be the last
time we would ever see our daughter alive.*

119

The coroner who dealt with the case over in Bogota was my second cousin. At my request, he spared me no detail. When Elena had become unwell on the way back to the airport after her two-week stay, the drug dealers had panicked and refused to put her on the flight back to London. They knew full well that the tightly wrapped packet of cocaine that she had swallowed had started to leak. My cousin assured me over and over that Elena was dead before they'd cut her stomach open to retrieve their assets. I'll never really know. But I do know that it was months before I stopped seeing that image in my head every night as I lay awake in bed. My baby girl. Cut open. Abandoned. Alone. Far away from the people who loved her most.

My cousin kindly attributed her death to misadventure on the death certificate, to spare us further anguish, and Elena's body was flown back to us for a small funeral. She's buried not far from Lower Haddelton. I often visit her to place flowers on her grave and fill her in on my news.

I never saw Anthony Pritchard again after that. Not until that evening in the foyer at Lottan Lodge.

Juan and I had talked long and hard about how we could track him down and hold him to account. But we'd known inside that it was all bravado. It would have been futile to try and connect him to our daughter's death. Anthony Pritchard had been a snake in the grass. And anyway, the wind had been knocked out of Juan's sails by then. In fact, he never really recovered from Elena's death. They said he'd had a heart attack when he died, but they were wrong. It had taken three years, but I knew that he'd died of a broken heart.

So, you see, when I stabbed Anthony Pritchard with that conveniently sharp steak knife, I had to do it twice. Once in the stomach for my beautiful daughter, and once in the heart for my beloved husband.

I'd started planning it as soon as I realised that Anthony had become a regular visitor to Lottan Lodge. Even before I'd worked out that he was still up to his old tricks. When I saw those young Latin American girls coming and going, I realised that I had no time to lose. I acquainted myself with exactly which CCTV cameras were working, and I knew that there were no cameras

120

on the emergency staircase. That was how I was going to get away with it.

My brisk evening walks turned into lengthy runs, far away, of course, from prying eyes in Lower Haddelton. I got very good at shuffling around the hotel. I practised that at home for a bit. I gradually stopped wearing make-up and putting colour in my greying hair, and kept complaining about my imaginary hip and back pain. If I was going to be dashing up and down several flights of stairs to commit a murder, I needed to be sure that I was well and truly out of the frame. I'm only sixty-three, but it wasn't long before everyone started seeing me as elderly and infirm. Isn't sixty meant to be the new forty these days? Well, as far as my colleagues at the hotel were concerned, I could have been nearly eighty.

As it was, building up my fitness and stamina, whilst appearing to age rapidly, turned out to be the easy part. The problem, that quiet Valentine's evening, was that every time I nipped up the stairs, there seemed to be someone else on that third-floor corridor having dealings with Anthony Pritchard. To use one of my favourite English expressions, it was like Piccadilly Circus up there.

First, that young Colombian girl came running out of the room in tears, and headed up in the other direction towards the lifts. I can't tell you how pleased I was to see that. I'd tried discreetly speaking to her on her previous visit, but she hadn't seemed to want to know.

I had to run downstairs again for a bit after that. I didn't want the kitchen staff to notice any long absences. I was making sure to chat madly to them all evening. I think they were getting a bit fed up with me, to be honest.

When I ran up the second time, after taking an order to the first floor, I could see Michael Winterbottom at Anthony's door for some reason. I had no idea what he was doing there. There hadn't been any Room Service orders for Room 304 as far as I knew. Yet again, I turned on my heel and headed back down the stairs to my stool in the kitchen.

The third time that I went up, after another Room Service request on the first floor, the coast seemed to be clear. This was my moment, I decided. I grabbed the knife that I'd hidden in a neighbouring room and knocked on the door of Room 304.

'What now? I've checked the envelope and it all seems to be in order,' Anthony had said impatiently, as he'd pulled open the door. Then he'd looked at me blankly. I was nothing to him, this man who had taken the lives of my daughter and my husband, and destroyed mine. There was no hesitation on my part. He had no time to react as I plunged the knife into his stomach. I waited patiently for him to fall backwards before I thrust the bloodied knife into his heart. I looked directly into his horrified eyes as he lay there. I wanted to see the pain in them as he faded away.

I'd just reached the fresh uniform and plastic rubbish bag that were waiting two rooms along, when I heard voices coming from the top of the stairs. I watched quietly in disbelief from the doorway as two women that I'd never seen before approached Anthony's door. They started knocking and calling his name. I had no idea who they were and what they were doing there, but I knew that I didn't want anybody else being accused of this murder. And, apart from anything else, they were standing directly between me and my escape route. I swept my hand along a row of empty coat hangers, making as much noise as I could, and it seemed to do the trick. They vanished as quickly as they had arrived. Precisely one minute later, I, too, was racing down those stairs and back into the kitchen, complaining about the rubbish I'd found next to a bin in the foyer. Rubbish that would be incinerated fairly shortly afterwards. Rubbish that included my plastic gloves, a blood-stained uniform, a couple of mobile phones and a wallet. I wanted Anthony Pritchard to lie dead, alone and unidentified for a while. Just like Elena.

I'd made sure to move the envelope of cash that I'd spotted into a very prominent position. Point the police in the right direction, hopefully. It didn't look like that much money really. Was that the price of a young girl's life?

I hadn't planned to be the first person to find Anthony's body the following morning. It had just worked out like that. I was rather relieved that Michael had witnessed it all. Though I do think I'd run a little bit too quickly out of the room. I was worried that I'd given myself away then. Especially when I started talking about fingerprints to Michael. I was treating the room as a crime

122

scene way before I should have. Michael was right, of course. Our guest could have just fainted or something, for all we knew.

Poor Michael. I felt dreadful when I found out that the police suspected him. He was a bit of a pain, but I certainly didn't want him to be arrested for a murder that he hadn't committed. I realised at that point that I had to let Bernardo Castillo know what had happened. I'd brought down the tray from outside his room at one point that evening. I didn't know exactly what was going on there, but I'd hoped that Bernardo could at least provide some sort of alibi for Michael. It seemed to work, thank goodness.

So, Anthony Pritchard is dead. And I am glad. I have no regrets. Yes, I've killed somebody. I've committed a murder. Believe you me, it's not the sort of thing that I usually do. I wouldn't normally harm a fly. I'm actually an extremely law-abiding person when I think about it. But I have no intention of paying for this crime while I walk this earth. I will answer to my Maker on this one. I'll let Him decide. And besides, I sense strongly that the Inspector on this case has felt the searing pain of loss. He understands what it is to grieve for a loved one. He would surely reason that, while extenuating circumstances might not necessarily justify my behaviour, they would certainly explain it. And he would take pity.

Of course, I have Sophie now, Elena's beautiful daughter. Initially, I'd really thought that she was trying to kill me, the way she kept creeping up on me like that. I was terrified that Anthony's associates had got to her; that they had somehow worked out the connection with Elena and had realised that it was me who had killed Anthony. So, of course, it was impossible to mention her behaviour to anyone without getting myself into trouble.

I can't put into words how wonderful it is to have the opportunity to spend time with Sophie. We have so much catching-up to do. Naturally, she doesn't need to know the true circumstances of her mother's death. And she will certainly never know how I dealt with her mother's murderer. But she will hear of all the love and laughter that once that existed in our lives. And she will always have my love, wherever she is in the world.

For now, that will be Paris with Fabian. She's beside herself with
excitement, and I am truly happy for them both.

But, if that handsome young French man EVER does anything
to hurt my beloved grand-daughter, well, all I can say is **bonne**
chance, *Fabian.*